the
DEAD
of CHACO
CANYON

the DEAD of CHACO CANYON

DONN CONN

TATE PUBLISHING & Enterprises

Published by Tate Publishing & Enterprises, LLC
127 E. Trade Center Terrace | Mustang, Oklahoma 73064 USA
1.888.361.9473 | www.tatepublishing.com

Tate Publishing is committed to excellence in the publishing industry. The company reflects the philosophy established by the founders, based on Psalm 68:11,
"The Lord gave the word and great was the company of those who published it."

Book design copyright © 2008 by Tate Publishing, LLC. All rights reserved.
Cover design by Lance Waldrop
Interior design by Kellie Southerland

Published in the United States of America

ISBN: 978-1-60696-906-9
1. Fiction   2. Action/Adventure
08.11.22

This book is dedicated to Marilyn,
my Joaquina.

DEADLY DISCOVERY

Will Scanlon checked his watch again. How long had it been since his friend had slithered through the crack in the canyon wall and vanished into the darkness of their discovery. His friend had taken their only flashlight and suggested only one of them enter the cave, just in case…

Will decided to wait another ten minutes before entering the cave in search of his friend. The sun was low on the horizon and it would soon be dark; they were several miles from the line shack where they had made camp.

Checking his watch for the tenth time in as many minutes, Will decided it was time. He had already spotted a pine tree nearby with some recent porcupine damage providing a source of pine pitch that he would use to light a torch. Taking a branch and his neckerchief wrapped in the sticky resin of the pine, he fashioned his torch. When it was lit he edged through the crack and into the chill wind blowing out of the cavern.

The passage was so small and narrow he had to crawl. He estimated he had crawled about forty or fifty yards before he could stand again. The farther into the cave he crawled, the colder it seemed. Finally he was able to stand and lifting his torch high above his head, he gazed upon the most astonishing, frightening, macabre sight his young eyes had ever seen.

He was so absorbed in the totally unbelievable scene before him, Will almost stumbled over the body. It was immediately obvious his friend was no longer a member of the living. His friend was in a sitting position and in his hand, within reach of another departed soul was a silver and turquoise bracelet. The eyes of Will's dead companion were filled with horror and his mouth gaped open. The flashlight lay on the ground creating ghostly shadows on the cave wall.

CHACO CANYON

Chaco Canyon, located twenty-six miles from the Blanco trading Post in northwestern New Mexico, continues to this day to confound archaeologists and anthropologists with its many unsolved mysteries.

The poorly-maintained dirt and gravel road takes one back in time to an amazing record of a culture and civilization that excites the imagination and creates a plethora of unanswered questions.

The Anasazi, the Ancient Ones who inhabited this area sometime between 900 and 1200 AD, were unsurpassed stonemasons, building structures with as many as four floors and eight hundred rooms. One can actually witness the progress of these masons' skills over the centuries of construction history.

Names such as Casa Chiquita, Kin Kletso, Pueblo del Arroyo, Pueblo Bonito, Chetro Ketl, Hungo Paui, Kin

Nahasbas and Una Vida adorn the many structures in the Canyon. Chetro Ketl is one of the more interesting buildings, with no less than eighteen Kivas, supporting the theory that Chaco was a religious center and gathering place for the Anasazi. The many subterranean rooms required the excavation of tons upon tons of earth, and involved thousands of man-hours of grueling labor. Archaeologists have determined that the timbers used for vigas (roof supports) came from as far away as fifty miles, and some were a foot in diameter. Based on the number of these used in the many structures in the Canyon, it amounted to a harvest of an approximate quarter million trees.

One must bear in mind that these artisans performed their construction feats without the benefit of tools as we know them. They had no metal tools whatsoever; no derricks to lift the heavy timbers and tons of stone to heights of four stories; not even shovels, as we think of shovels, to excavate the many kivas found in the Canyon.

This ancient culture also boasted considerable knowledge of astronomy, and the Sun Dagger of Fajada Butte is testimony to this fact. Three monoliths were positioned on a mesa top in the exact position to capture a solar shadow on a circular petroglyph at the precise time of the summer solstice, an amazing feat. In addition, however, the windows of several of the buildings also capture moonlight and sunlight to mark both summer and winter solstice on the walls. These ancient calendars were used to mark and record religious festivities, as well as for agricultural guidelines. One wonders at the many hours invested in watching the heavens to acquire this knowledge and then to apply it to the benefit of the community.

In the 1970's aerial photography, and later satellite pictures, confirmed what archaeologist suspected a road network fanning out from Chaco in random directions for hundreds of miles … a road network thirty feet wide, as straight as a surveyor's line, with total disregard for terrain such as steep canyon walls. This culture did not have horses or wheels, nothing but pedestrian travel. Why then a roadway thirty feet wide, and why and how a roadway stretching as straight as an arrow for a hundred miles.

Archaeologists estimate that, during the three hundred or so years that Chaco Canyon was inhabited, the apex of the population may have been as many as thirty thousand souls. Think of the agricultural support it must have taken to sustain a community of these numbers.

So many unanswered questions regarding Chaco Canyon, but perhaps the most confounding is the Mystery of the Dead.

Based on the estimated population, it is reasonable to accept as fact that thousands of those Anasazi lived out their life span and died. Where are the burial sites of those thousands of expired pilgrims? Archaeological sifting through ash pits tends to confirm the theory that this particular culture did not use cremation as a disposal of human remains. Where then is the ancient burial ground of the Anasazi of Chaco Canyon? One question begets another. The Dead of Chaco Canyon … a mystery yet to be solved.

WILL SCANLON

Will Scanlon, now twenty three, was born and raised in Lakeville, just south of Minneapolis. He had grown into a strapping lad of six foot and weighed about one ninety. He had thick, wavy, dark brown hair and a thick bushy mustache to match. His dark brown eyes smiled, radiating confidence and well being. His father had always encouraged him to go into sales, as he was convinced Will could sell a drowning man a glass of water.

Will had just completed a four-year tour with the United States Marine corps, and was enrolling in college at the University of New Mexico. He had had only two colleges in mind when he settled on UNM, the other being the University of Wyoming at Laramie. UNM won out primarily due to his sister's lobbying for her old almamater.

His sister Jennifer, six years his senior, had attended

UNM while working on her Master's degree before going on to Stanford to earn her Doctorate in Anthropology. She was currently the assistant curator at the Museum of Natural History in Minneapolis and working on a research paper about the Southwest Anasazi. Much of her research took her to the immense archaeological site at Chaco Canyon in New Mexico.

Their father had been an Archaeologist of world-wide recognition. He was an accepted authority in the field of Egyptology. The children, growing up in this environment, had been exposed to and developed and interest in both archaeology and anthropology. They had also enjoyed much travel abroad, which expanded their horizons and provided them with a maturity and sophistication beyond their peers.

Will had grown up sharing his father's love of the field and stream. Under his father's tutelage, he had become both an accomplished fly fisherman, and a considerable wing shot of upland game and water fowl. His father had died two years ago and Will would probably always miss these outings, especially during the fall and at Thanksgiving.

Will's mother was enjoying good health and still living in the home place in Lakeville. In her mid-fifties, she stayed active and busy with volunteer work at the hospital and her church. His mother was a mild mannered woman, and neither he nor his sister could ever remember her raising her voice in anger. This easy going, mild manner, and acceptance of the world and its shortcomings had been passed on to Will. He seldom seemed to get angry and had patience beyond comprehension.

Will was standing in line at the registration office when he first met Alan Savage. Alan was explaining to the registrar he would be pursuing a degree in Archaeology and needed some direction. As the clerk was entering information into her computer, Will introduced himself

"Couldn't help but overhear you're going after a degree in Archaeology. So am I. My name's Will Scanlon."

"My name's Alan Savage, nice to meet you. Where's home?"

"Lakeville, Minnesota, just south of Minneapolis, where's home for you?"

"Believe it or not, I'm a New Mexico native, born and reared west of here out of Grants."

This conversation was interrupted by the woman assisting with the enrollment.

Later as Will was stumbling about the campus trying to get his bearings he ran into Alan Savage again.

Alan asked, "How about lunch, I know a sandwich shop on Central that for two bucks you can bust a gut?"

Will readily agreed and off they went. Will was feeling good about making an acquaintance and not seeming so alone.

Alan was every bit as tall as Will but stouter and outweighed Will by several pounds. Alan also had dark thick hair and a mustache to match and could have passed for Will's brother. Alan was dressed in Levis and boots and a large silver buckle on a carved leather belt. A white dress shirt was fancied up with a silver and turquoise bolo tie, and a black Stetson with a wide brim finished it off. The hat was sweat stained and had seen considerable wear. It was obvious to Will that Alan was no Rexall Ranger with round toed boots that had never seen a corral. Alan was in, Will's mind, the epitome of what a real ranch hand should look like.

Enroute to the sandwich shop Alan explained. "I'm meeting a friend who will be joining us for lunch. You'll like her, she's very special."

As they entered the sandwich shop, some one called, "Alan, I'm over here."

They made their way over to the table where Sandy was sitting and Alan introduced Will.

"Will, this is Sandy Yazzie, she and I went to school together, and her brothers work on our ranch. Sandy, meet Will Scanlon, he's going to be in some of my classes and he's from Minnesota."

In the course of eating lunch and visiting with his two new friends, Will found out that; Alan's father owned a very large ranch out of Grants, and Sandy and Alan had gone to high school together and her two older brothers worked on the Diamond G ranch belonging to Alan's father.

Sandy was a Navajo, about five two and weighed over two hundred pounds. But she had the most beautiful face framed with black, shiny, long hair that came down to her silver and turquoise concho belt. Her conversation was both animated and interesting. He was taken by the warmth and sincerity both she and Alan had extended to this stranger.

Good luck upon good luck. Before the luncheon was finished it had been determined that Will could move in with Sandy and Alan. They had rented a small three bedroom house just off campus and were looking for another roommate. Alan and Sandy had a very close relationship as they had grown up together almost as brother and sister, and in the months to come Will became a welcome member of this trio.

School was great and Will was fast at learning study methods. Things were working out at the apartment with an established pattern of sharing the household chores and expenses. They were a compatible group. Will was more than thankful for his good fortune.

Just before the Thanksgiving break Alan asked Will

if he would like to join his family on the ranch for the holiday.

Will couldn't have been more pleased. His response was immediate and positive with sincere thanks. Thanksgiving had always been his favorite holiday. He and his father had usually gone goose hunting Thanksgiving morning to return mid-afternoon to a house filled with the grandest smells of turkey, mince meat pie and a roaring fire place. Memories that would never dim with the passing of time.

THE RANCH

The Wednesday before Thanksgiving Will and Alan headed west out of Albuquerque on I-40 to Grants, where they then turned south. They hadn't gone far out of Grants when they turned off the highway onto a dirt road that followed an arroyo for several miles. They continued west across several cattle guards before finally he could see the first out-buildings and main ranch house just this side of a large stand of timber. A large barn was set below and to the south of the main building with other outbuildings, one obviously a bunk house, and extensive pens and corrals, some with cattle and some with horses. A beautiful sight on a warm fall afternoon with the lengthening shadows creeping eastward.

Alan braked his four wheel drive pick-up in front of the main house, and before he shut off the engine his mother and father were out the door.

Mrs. Savage was an attractive, rather petite. gray haired woman with an apron covering her faded levi shirt and jeans. Her jeans were worn over a pair of high heeled red boots.

Mr. Savage could have been a brother to the film star Gary Cooper. He was tall and thin with an inseam that would allow him to step over a four strand barbed-wire fence with ease. His face was weather beaten, darkly tanned and wrinkled, testifying to the many years of wind and sun. Crows feet gave his eyes the impression that they were smiling. His gait. with those long legs, was almost lumbering giving the appearance that his upper body was swaying. Like Mrs. Savage, he was wearing faded levis, a white shirt and a bolo tie. His handshake, as was that of Mrs. Savage, was strong and welcoming.

Mrs. Savage was the first to speak, after giving Alan a long and lengthy hug, "welcome to the Diamond G, Will."

Mr. Savage said, "Add my welcome to that, young man. Always glad to host Alan's friends. Gives us a chance to find out just what's really goin' on down at that school. Can't always count on Sandy tellin' us anything about Alan, a habit she got into, way back when they was little folk."

Mr. Savage picked up their duffels, escorted them into the house and showed Will his room located in one of the new wings. Placing Will's duffel on the bed, he added, "get settled and join us in the den and we'll have time for a Bruja Brew before dinner."

When Will joined them in the den he marveled at the size and decor of the Savage home.

The ranch house was native stone with a large glassed-in porch area and several wings extending out on each side of the original and main house. There were two fire places, one on each end of the large den, each of them with a roaring fire, crackling and emitting the pleasant smell of burning cedar.

There were four large Navajo rugs covering a large portion of the native flagstone floor. The rugs were Two Gray Hills and Ganado Red. These were some of the most expensive and finest efforts of the Navajo weavers and were usually displayed on the walls, not used in their originally intended utilitarian place on the floor. Conversely, there were several rugs on the walls that were obviously Mexican in origin.

Also on the walls were several mounted heads. One, a trophy Elk with seven points on one side and eight on the other. There were also several four point mule deer, and a black bear rug with head displaying a mouth full of large teeth.

On the south wall hung an old pair of bat wing chaps with the Diamond G brand burned on each leg, and a pair of old spurs with Mexican rowels and engraved silver jingle-bobs.

The furniture was massive heavy oak, and the sofa and two large chairs were covered with sorrel and white cow hide. The curtains were thick woven, off white, with soft blue and gray Indian designs complementing the many rugs.

A wide entrance on the east side of the room opened into a large well-appointed kitchen. An island in the middle was surrounded by every major appliance designed to accommodate the finest of chefs. A large door on the south end of the kitchen opened into a walk-in freezer with sides of beef, pork, and venison hanging, and several dressed wild turkeys. One end of the walk-in pantry was dedicated to a wine cellar that would shame many a fine restaurant.

Will was totally impressed with the home and life style Alan and his family apparently enjoyed. But as Alan was to share with him later, " It didn't just happen." A lot of hard work and a lot of lean years when drought and a down cattle market had made things tough. Alan's father was still up before sunrise and often not back to the barn before sundown.

Alan's grandfather had put the original ranch together with not much more than a wagon load of barbed wire and fifty head of cows. Mr. Savage had never been out of the state of New Mexico. He married Sarah when he was nineteen and she was seventeen. They lived in a small adobe house just west of the barn in those early years. It no longer stands and only a trace of the foundation remains.

Sarah's family was the nearest neighbors to the Savage ranch back then. Their ranch was almost twenty miles to the south and east.

The second year they were married, Sarah gave birth to a little girl. They named her Virginia after Sarah's mother. She was killed in a fall from a horse when she was only seven. They still grieved over the loss of this delightful child. It was several years after that, that Alan was born. Alan was named Alan Simpson Savage, Simpson being his mother's maiden name and Alan being his grandfather's name. He had numerous scraps over the years, thanks to those initials.

Thanksgiving morning Will woke to a bright and sunny day with the smell of bacon coming from the kitchen. He hurried his shower and shave, fearing he would be late for breakfast. He followed the smell of bacon into the kitchen. The first one to greet him was Sandy.

"Good morning, Mr. Sleeper, you look surprised to see me. I drove over from the reservation this morning, it's just down the road. I always celebrate the holidays here at the ranch. You'll get to meet my brothers at dinner. They're out working with the rest of the men. It appears only eastern dudes get to sleep in and have a late breakfast."

Mrs. Savage, dressed in skirt and blouse and beautiful Indian jewelry, said, "Don't pay any attention to Sandy, Will, Her bark is as harmless as a coyote without teeth. Sit down and tell me how, and how many, and I'll fix your eggs while your roomy pours you a cup of coffee."

It was obvious to Will that Sandy was indeed family, and he enjoyed listening to the two women sharing woman talk as he wolfed down his eggs and bacon wrapped in tortillas with green chili sauce. What a great way to commence a holiday, he thought.

Sandy took Will for a walk about the property and down to the barn where Alan and his dad were busy shoeing a horse. They were both wearing heavy shotgun chaps and manure-covered boots with spurs. They both took turns shaming Will about his long stay in the sack and suggested Sandy check him for bed sores so they could apply some teat baum, which would surely be a healing solution.

Will volunteered to Mr. Savage, that there had been more than one occasion when Sandy and Alan had found it difficult to quit the sheets of a morning. It was obvious that this family enjoyed humor and no one was immune to the occasional ragging.

After a quick lesson in the art of a farrier and several failed attempts to drive the nail correctly through the hoof, Will surrendered the hammer and resumed the role of spectator.

Two horses and considerable conversation later, the four of them headed for the house in anticipation of the Thanksgiving feast awaiting them.

They were enjoying some of Mr. Savage's wine selection when Sandy's brothers entered the room. Sandy jumped up to introduce them, but was too late, as Mrs. Savage coming through the kitchen took an arm of each of them and said, "Will, I'd like you to meet the pride of the Yazzie clan, Jason and Justin, in that order."

The boys looked enough alike to be twins, but there were two years separating them, Jason being the oldest at twenty nine. Each was no more than five seven or eight. Both wore their hair long, Jason's tied up in a bun, Justin's in a long braid down his back. They were wearing plaid western cut shirts with pearl button snaps, new unfaded jeans, and western boots. Both had worked for the Diamond G as long as they could remember. Both lived in the bunk house and took most of their meals here in Mrs. Savage's kitchen. Jason had been married once and lived on the reservation, but his wife had gone off to California with a dentist who had worked at the clinic on the reservation.

Will liked them both right away. They had firm handshakes and looked him in the eye, which is an absolute departure from the Navajo way. Among themselves the Navajo do not look directly at a person. It is considered extremely rude to do so.

When Mrs. Savage called them all to dinner, Mr. Savage gave a long and somewhat emotional grace as he thanked God for family, friends, health, and material blessings beyond their deserving.

The Thanksgiving feast was everything Will expected, turkey and dressing, both white and sweet potatoes, cranberry sauce, home made rolls, and both pumpkin and mince meat pies.

After dinner Mrs. Savage played the piano and Alan the guitar and they all joined in singing songs Will hadn't heard since high school, and some he hadn't heard at all. They all seemed to know all the verses and Alan and his Father could harmonize and it was the grandest Thanksgiving holiday, Will could remember.

It was all over too soon, and Sunday after joining the Savage family at the local United Methodist Church in Grants, Will and Alan loaded up the pickup and headed back to Albuquerque and their studies.

Mr. & Mrs. Savage asked Will to keep Alan out of trouble and invited him to come back anytime, with or without Sandy and Alan. Will felt he had really found a family in New Mexico and was having feelings that had been dormant for years.

ZUNI

It was just a little after 7 a.m. and the phone was ringing for the seventh time when Sandy finally picked it up. "Yes , we're up."

The voice on the other end said, "Sandy, is that you? This is Billy Otero; I'm looking for Alan."

"Good morning, Billy, hang on; I'll see if he's out of the shower." Then yelling into the back of the apartment. "Alan it's Billy Otero, for you."

"Tell him to wait while I slip on my levis," was the reply from the back bathroom.

Minutes later, "Billy amigo, Alan es aqui, que pasa?"

"Damn it Alan, you know I don't speak Spanish. why must you always do that? Why can't you learn just a little Zuni for a change?"

Alan apologized and asked, "What can I do for you, Billy?"

"Apology accepted," said Billy. "How about driving up to the Pueblo this week for the Shalako ceremonies?"

The Shalako ceremonies had always been one of Alan's favorite Indian ceremonies and dances. After a brief consideration, Alan responded, "We were just home several weeks ago for Thanksgiving, but if I can bring our friend Will Scanlon along, I'll graciously accept."

"Bring Sandy along if that crazy Navajo isn't concerned about too much exposure to real honest to goodness Native American culture."

Alan laughed and offered, "If that's really the way you want me to extend the invitation, I'll repeat it verbatim."

It was settled then, and Alan rang off and hollered to his roommates that he had just put a three day hole in the rest of their week.

Sandy declined the invitation as she had several tests she was not prepared for.

Will accepted with some degree of reluctance. His studies had suffered attention during the Thanksgiving break.

Alan went on to explain that Billy Otero was a Zuni, and like Sandy and her brothers, was also part of the extended Savage family. Billy's father had worked for the Diamond G until his death about three years ago. Billy had come to work on the ranch shortly thereafter, when he was eighteen. As there wasn't enough work year around, Billy only worked on the ranch about seven months out of the year.

He was a hard worker and good with livestock, and the Yazzie brothers had taken to him right away. He and Sandy had an even closer relationship. In fact Mrs. Savage would encourage this relationship every chance she got. The fact that one was Zuni, and the other Navajo, didn't disturb her in the least. Her argument for her continued meddling, to both Alan and his father, was that, "It's no different than a Protestant marrying a Catholic."

Alan and Will loaded up the pickup and left right after breakfast, after a call to the ranch to assure they would be expected for lunch.

Another warm reception for Will and another of Sarah's fine meals was brightening up a cold and gray December day. After lunch Mr. Savage invited Will into the den and offered to provide him with a "poor man's quick and dirty overview of the Zuni people."

"The Zuni Reservation is just up the road to Gallup and then a jog to the southwest. The Zuni Pueblo is the most populous of the Pueblos, numbering around eight thousand souls. In 1692 when the Spaniard de Vargas was busy reconquering New Mexico, the Zuni were living in the shadow of 'Towayalane' their sacred Corn Mountain. But shortly after, they moved a short distance and began building their present pueblo, including the old site of Halona, on the Zuni River." Mr. Savage continued, explaining, "The reservation covers nearly 410,000 acres."

"The Pueblo is divided into the north people and the south people; the summer people and the winter people. The summer cacique or jefe, is the speaker to the sun. The winter cacique is the rain priest of the north. There are about thirteen different clans named after the different totems. They are not strictly a matriarchal society. The lineage of both mother and father are important in that they dictate the different social and ceremonial duties. Ritual and ceremonies become the responsibilities of the father's household and economic responsibilities fall on the mother's household and lineage."

"A Zuni is born into a household, and that determines his clan affiliation and kinship status. a number of the clans are associated with the six directions - the four cardinal points of the compass and the zenith and the nadir. The six kivas of the Pueblo represent these six directions. The Zuni kivas, unlike some of the Rio Grande group which are round and below ground, are rectangular in shape and above ground."

"The economic unit, or household, is the family based on matriarchal residence. These are a series of adjoining rooms owned by the women, since descent is matrilineal. On ritual occasions the men return to their natal household to carry out important ceremonial duties."

"While the clans have considerable significance, they have no social or political function. The Zuni speaking people have been occupying their present area for over eight hundred years, according to archaeological evidence. The Zuni people claim as ancestors the Anasazi of Chaco Canyon.'

While Mr. Savage paused in his dissertation, Will asked, "Where in the world did you get all this information?"

Mr. Savage responded, "Will, I have been a student of the Native Americans of the southwest for many years. It has been a fascinating pursuit of knowledge about a fascinating subject."

He continued, as Will sat and listened spellbound. "The Zuni are famous for their carved fetishes. The carvings were originally used in religious ceremonies and were very sacred. The woman of each household and her brothers were responsible for looking after these sacred objects."

"The Zuni language is unique and is probably derived from Penutian stock which is probably related to Tanoan. The Pueblo people have several different language groups; those being, Tewa, Tiwa, and Towa, which are related tongues perhaps deriving from a common linguistic family known as Tanoan. The Keres spoken by some of the Rio Grande Pueblos is distinct from the inclusive Indian languages of North America. Evidence indicates that Keres has been spoken in the southwest for eons."

"Both the Navajo and Apache language are probably a derivation of the Athabascan language group. And that, Will, should be enough of an introduction to this subject. I don't want to fill your young head with more information than you really want to know."

"On the contrary, Mr. Savage, I agree with you, it's a fascinating subject, and I thank you for sharing it with me."

Will thanked Mrs. Savage for another grand meal and he and Alan loaded their gear in the pickup and started up the road towards Gallup.

Before they had crossed the second cattle guard, Will shared with Alan that in just this short time he felt as if he had been a part of the Savage family forever.

Alan volunteered that his parents seemed to have that effect on people, take for example the Yazzies and Billy, whom he would soon meet.

BILLY OTERO

They left I-40 at Gallup and were heading south on Highway 602. As they drove through Gallup Alan had promised Will that next August he would bring him to the grandest rodeo in the world. He said Gallup hosted the entire Indian nation every summer in one of the most colorful and authentic presentations of the Native American cultures.

About eighteen miles out of Gallup is the town of Vanderwagon. It was originally named White Water but the name was changed in 1949 to commemorate Andrew Vanderwagon, a missionary who in 1897 preached the gospel to the Zuni and Navajos. By the time it took Alan to tell all this to Will the town lay in the dust behind them.

It was turning colder and the sun was setting as they turned into the Pueblo. They drove in the near dark down a rutty dirt road past a row of one-story row houses and pulled up alongside a yellow pick-up with a stock rack.

Alan said, "Billy's here, that's his pick-up."

Before they were out of the truck, Billy Otero had come through the door of the house, opened the door on Alan's side of the truck and all but pulled him out of the cab.

Here again, as were the Yazzie brothers with their anglo friends, was a departure from the accepted tribal social mores. Billy hugged Alan and said, "If you get much uglier, Alan, you'll never have any grandchildren for your folks."

Alan's response was immediate, "Not to worry Billy, they think your children will be their grandchildren. Come meet my roomy, Will Scanlon. Will, meet Billy Otero, the ugliest Indian on the reservation."

Billy Otero was a handsome man of twenty three or two, about five foot nine, and weighed in the neighborhood of one seventy five or eighty.

As could be expected, he had dark brown eyes and long dark black hair which he wore down to his shoulders. He was wearing a panama Stetson with a bull-dogger block, that seemed out of place in the winter; a red plaid flannel shirt and time-worn levis held up by a beaded belt with a silver and turquoise buckle. His high-heeled boots were totally lacking of any maintenance or polish. They were the color of bleached doe skin and were run over at the heels.

He seemed to smile with his mouth and eyes at the same time and appeared to be silently laughing all the time. It was obvious to Will, that he enjoyed life and people.

Taking Will's extended hand, he grasped it firmly and said, "How did a fine fellow like you, get mixed up with this ugly anglo?" All this with a grin, as he looked back over his shoulder, to observe Alan's response. " Don't mention to any of my family that you know him. If they ask, tell them you picked him up on the road."

At this, Alan interrupted, "His family has known me for years, and if truth be known, I am probably more welcome here than he is."

They all three were still laughing over these friendly insults as they entered the house.

The room they entered was large and the warmth from the fireplace smelling of pinon and cedar smoke, along with light from two kerosene lamps, made for a welcome atmosphere.

Standing near the fire place holding her two-year old son was Joaquina, Billy's younger sister. She put the boy down and came across the room to hug Alan.

Alan, while still embracing Joaquina, turned to Will and said, "Will, meet Billy's sister Joaquina, the most beautiful woman this side of the sacred mountain."

Will caught his breath. He was sure his mouth was hanging open and he was quite certain he looked stupid. For indeed, standing before him was the most beautiful woman he had ever seen. All he could do was to nod slightly and smile.

Joaquina was about five four with eyes that seemed almost black they were so dark, with hair to match, worn nearly down to her waist. In the glow of the lanterns both her eyes and hair were shining with a luminescence almost ethereal. When she smiled, her teeth were so white they reflected the artificial light bathing the room. Like her brother's, her smile and eyes seemed to be laughing together at some secret piece of humor. When she spoke, Will's instant reaction was to recall the phrase, "The lilt of Irish laughter." Her voice was soft and melodious and yet could be described as husky. She was wearing a colorful long peasant skirt and a low cut

Spanish-style white blouse that could not begin to conceal the voluptuous beauty it covered.

She smiled at Will, nodded slightly, and said, "Welcome to our home, friend of Alan's."

All Will could manage was a slight nod and smile in return; afraid that if he opened his mouth at this point he would probably stutter or squeak.

Both Alan and Billy were aware of the impact Joaquina's beauty had had on Will. They had both witnessed this same reaction on many occasions.

Just as this awkward situation was about to become more awkward, Billy's Grandmother, Maria Otero, entered the room.

As she did so, she looked at the three young men in the center of the room and stopped dead in her tracks, threw both arms in the air, cried out something in Zuni and retreated to the kitchen.

Joaquina reached down and picked up little Joaquin, and rushed into the kitchen to determine the cause of her Grandmother's strange behavior.

Grandmother Maria was sitting at the kitchen table with her head in her hands, sobbing quietly.

Joaquina asked, "Grandmother, what is it, what have you seen?"

Maria Otero was probably in her eighties. She was a famous maker of the Zuni fetishes. Her family had been responsible for one of the Shalako Kachina masks for generations. She was a healer, a seer. There were over four hundred plants and shrubs on this reservation and Maria knew every one by name along with its' healing or poisonous properties. She knew the tribal history as it had been handed down over the years. She had been blessed, or cursed, with the "Far Seeing Eye."

Grandmother Maria took Joaquina's hand in hers, looked up at her and said, "Joaquina my child, I am wrong to burden you with this knowledge, but I cannot carry this heavy load all by myself. You must never repeat what I am sharing with you now."

Those fine young men who are in this house tonight… Two of them will not live to see the snow melt in the high country. They will be gone before the Coyote whelps have been weaned. This I have seen. I would not have told you, if it were not so."

Joaquina had been privy on more than one occasion to her Grandmother's predictions. She knew beyond any doubt that her powers to observe future events were accurate and absolute.

"Tell me Grandmother, which of these young men will see the Aspen turn?'

"That burden you must not bear, my child; trust me now."

Joaquina returned to the other room and looking at these three fine young men and wondered about the brevity and uncertainty of life.

"Please excuse Grandmother, she needed to attend to something on the stove. Billy, make your friends at home and keep Joaquin busy while I help in the kitchen."

With that she returned to the kitchen to be with her Grandmother and the frightening thoughts her Grandmother's announcement had created.

Grandmother Maria again took Joaquina's hands in hers and looked deeply into her eyes and said, "Joaquina, my child, hear me now as I speak. You know from your childhood teachings that our clan, and our house, are the caretakers of the ancient Shalako Kachina mask. We have been instructed and have carried out those responsibilities of caretaker. When the Shalako Wo'le came to observe our handling of these responsibilities, he found several broken buckskin strings on the Mask. It is known that in the past when such responsibilities were not handled properly a terrible thing was visited on the family. I fear that our clan will be punished. Now go, be with our guests and speak no more of this. Do as I say, go now."

SHALAKO

The Shalako ceremony that Will had been invited to observe is an annual ceremony that takes place in early December. The are six identical Shalako and each one with his alternate (Anuthlona Shalako) forms a pair of Shalako Dancers.

One pair is drawn from each of the six kivas. The effigy mask is so large it requires two person alternating to present the impersonation.

The Shalako with the mask reaches nine feet in height and has a large bird like beak that they clack repeatedly. This kachina is probably the most remarkable of all the effigies.

The twelve selected Shalako impersonators are obligated for an entire year. They must attend numerous training sessions, learn traditional prayers and plant prayer sticks once a month for ten months. At the end of which follows a forty-nine day period when prayer sticks are planted every ten days. At the end of this period, the ten Koyemci (mudheads) appear and announce the coming of the Shalako and then the Koyemci go into retreat for eight days.

Four days later the twelve Shalako impersonators go into their four day retreat.

At the beginning of the Shalako ceremony ten masked Koyemci come the across the plain from the abiding place of the Gods and announce that in four days the Kachinas representing the Kok-kos (Gods) will return to the village after their summer absence and that in eight days Shalako will begin. They make obscene gestures and vulgar speeches during this part of the ceremony.

The Koyemci (Mudheads) are the most dangerous of all. If you touch a Koyemci while he has his paint on you will surely go crazy. They carry the sacred butterfly Lahacoma in their drum to make people follow them. Anyone who follows Lahacoma will go crazy.

The organization of the Koyemci differs from other clown groups in that they are not a fraternity. The ten Koyemci are appointed by the priests and, like the Shalako, they also serve for a full year.

At least four societies provide men for this position so that no group will have to perform more often that every four years. The other Zuni Clowns belong to the Newekwe and Galaxy fraternities.

The Koyemci, often called Mudheads, are always ten in number; their masks are similar but the accouterments and costumes have minute differences. These changes in costumes indicate a different name and role. They are all painted with pink clay from the Sacred Lake. The bumps or knobs protruding from the masks contain important seeds from different crops.

The different Koyemci are: AwanTatchu (Father),

Eshotsi (Bat), Pekwin (Sun Speaker), Nalashi (Aged One), Isepasha (Glum One), Kalutsi (Infant), Posuki (pouter), Tsathlashi (Old Youth), Apithlashi'wanni (Bow Priest), and Muyapona (Vain One).

They act in reverse of that which their name implies. For example the Bat is terrified of the dark , and Posuki the Pouter laughs hilariously at everything.

At the end of the retreat for the Shalako and Koyemci the ceremony continues. On this evening Shulawitsi's fire at White Rock signals the Shalako Wo'le that it is time to bring out the Shalako Masks.

On this last day of retreat the Wo'le take the Masks to White Rock. Then they return and wash the hair of the Impersonators who then go to the house of their Mother and have their hair put up; they then gather up their prayer sticks, return to White Rock and put on their masks.

In the evening the Shalako plant prayer sticks at the bottom of Greasy Hill and proceed to the field South of the river. At this location is the shrine of Hepatina. From this point they race towards the northeast clacking their beaks.

From this point a myriad of lengthy and precise rituals take place, after which each Shalako returns to its designated house.

Here again precise rituals are observed, lasting until dawn. Another day of exacting ritual takes place until the Shalako plant their final prayer sticks at the White Rocks and return to the village sans masks to have their hair washed again. This concludes their year long obligation. At this time the Wo'le gather the masks and return them with continued ceremony to their assigned houses to await next year's ceremony.

JOAQUINA

After a meal of mutton stew, tortillas and frijoles, topped off with Indian bread, Joaquina invited Will to walk down to the river with her. Handing her son to Billy, she grabbed her shawl and opened the door for Will.

It was surprisingly warm for a December night. A cloudless sky was full of stars close enough to touch. The brightness of a rising moon now beginning to peek over the sacred Corn Mountain.

The wind had died with sunset, and it was a dead calm that accentuated the noise of the crusted snow and dry leaves. The hoot of an owl somewhere in the distance broke the silence.

As they started toward the river, Joaquina wrapped her arm in Will's and they continued arm in arm without speaking, simply drinking in the beauty of this night and each others company.

Will was full of a satisfying warmth of soul that he could not explain. It was as if the only thing that mattered was this serene moment, and he had a desire to lock this time in space and never lose it. It was a long, long way from Minnesota. Here he was, in an environment that seemed as if he had stepped back in space a thousand years. His mind and thought seemed in a time warp.

He was brought back to the present by the sound of Joaquina's soft warm voice asking, "Tell me Will Scanlon, what do you think of all this Zuni pageantry and ceremony?"

He stopped and looked into here eyes and said in a hushed voice, fearing he may interrupt the silence of this beautiful night, "Joaquina, I couldn't begin to describe my feelings right now. I feel as if we were in a church and to speak would almost be irreverent. I feel the beauty of this night and the presence of a beautiful woman. I cannot recall such feelings before. I am reluctant to say anything for fear it may destroy the magic of this moment."

Joaquina reached out and took both his hands in hers and said, "I too feel that this is a special scene in my walk through time, that I will hold in my heart and treasure."

With those words she inclined her head towards his. His response was natural and predictable. He took her in his arms and kissed her long and tenderly. Her lips were warm and inviting. Will felt consumed by a burning desire.

They stood there in each other's arms for the longest time, savoring this moment until finally Will broke the silence.

"Joaquina, what have you done to me? It's as if you have wrapped yourself around my very heart and soul. What's it been, three hours at most since I met you? And it's as if my entire life to this point has been heading for this very moment. . Almost as if it had been ordained.

It is quite frightening, to say the least. I am not used to being possessed by my feelings, out of control as it were. I need to know where this is headed. You have a son. Where is his father? Why is his name Otero, the same as yours? Perhaps I am being foolish, presumptuous, and out of line.

Joaquina waited for what seemed to Will an eternity before responding. "Like you, I have strong feelings that I cannot account for. Feelings that I have not felt before; at least not this intense. The questions you ask need to be answered. Joaquin's father left shortly after he was born and went to Arizona to work in a mine. He has never returned. Grandmother Maria told me several months ago that he was no longer of this world. She said she saw him nearly covered with sand in a dry wash in the desert outside of Phoenix. He had been murdered in a knife fight during a drinking spree. His son was the result of a single indiscretion by a young and foolish young girl. He was a handsome, and perhaps reckless young man, but he didn't deserve such a death."

"Joaquina, I know so very little about your customs and I know our worlds are miles apart. But I know as sure as summer sky is blue I love you will all my heart. Who must I see and what must I do to arrange the proper courting of this Zuni woman?"

Will Scanlon, I know so little about you. Only that you are a friend of Alan's and attend the University. But you also have wrapped yourself around my heart. It is not necessary to seek permission to court me. But hear this and do not ask me to explain. If, after the snow melts in the high country and the coyote whelps are weaned, you come to me and ask, I will become yours, and we will glory in the gold of the aspen leaves in Autumn."

They remained there along-side the river in each other's arms, each with their own thoughts, each caught up in the magic of the moment and this spectacular night that was so different from any other.

Finally, they turned and walked back to the house in silence; back to the fellowship of family and friends.

As they came through the door, little Joaquin lay asleep in his Uncle Billy's lap with his little kachina doll held tight in his hands.

To both Alan and Billy, it was immediately obvious that during their lengthy absence this couple had become something more than a new acquaintance.

As Grandmother Maria entered the room, Joaquina tried desperately to determine any indication of feelings on her Grandmother's face as she looked at Will and Joaquina. But to no avail. Grandmother's countenance reflected nothing one way or another.

Grandmother offered them coffee or tea and suggested Joaquina put her son to bed and then explain further to their guests the ceremonies they would be observing.

Alan had been whistling along with the country-western songs on the pick-up radio. Will was silently staring out the window. It had been almost half an hour now since they had said good-by to the Otero family and turned onto the highway.

Will reached over and turned down the volume on the radio and asked Alan, "When does the snow melt in the high country and when do the coyotes wean their whelps?"

"What in blazes are you asking? What kind of questions are those?" Alan asked as he took his eyes off the road and looked in amazement at his friend.

"You sit there in a trance for a half hour and then ask when does the snow melt in the high country? I know you're obviously smitten by that Zuni girl, but surely you're not going to wax poetic on me."

"Damn it, Alan, I'm serious. Joaquina said that if I still wanted her after the snow melts in the high country and the coyote whelps are weaned, she would be mine."

Alan looked at him thoughtfully before answering and then said, "If you're really serious, I suggest you give a lot of thought to the gulf that separates your two cultures. I'm not saying that a strong love, if it indeed exists, can't bridge the gap. But the situation deserves some considerable.... ." He never finished that thought but went on to answer Will's question. "Sometime the snow lasts on the peaks until mid-summer. I reckon if the pups came in late winter, about the time the calves are dropping, they'd quit the teat by about the time the snow melts above timber-line."

It was another twenty silent miles before either spoke again. Then Will broke the silence. "When does the aspen turn gold?"

THE VALENTINE

The heater in Billy Otero's pick-up wasn't throwing out that much heat and Joaquina suggested to Billy, "We should have taken one of the Savage trucks for this trip. I always wonder that your old truck can make such a trip, and I'm not so sure it isn't warmer outside,"

Billy and Joaquina had left the Pueblo before dawn and stopped by the Diamond G enroute to Albuquerque. They enjoyed a quick visit with Mrs. Savage, while they ate a piece of her warm apple pie, just out of the oven. They were taking along two more of her pies to deliver to the students and some laundry Alan and Will had left at the ranch.

Billy had pulled alongside the gas tank near the barn and filled the tank in his pick-up and a five gallon can as his fuel gauge had broken some time back. He was to pick up some veterinary supplies in Albuquerque, along with some salt blocks. They were getting ready to move the bred heifers down closer to the main ranch, anticipating they would start dropping calves soon. Mr. Savage had predicted, "That as sure as dogs bark, the heifers will wait for the worst storm to start dropping calves." It never seemed to fail, and what a world for those calves to enter, with blowing snow and the glass falling below the zero mark.

Joaquina had asked to go along with Billy, under the pretense of delivering some of Grandmother Maria's fetishes to the Indian Cultural Center for consignment. When Bill had mentioned he would be making a trip to Albuquerque in February, Joaquina jumped at the chance to see Will Scanlon again. Billy was glad for the company, and lately he really enjoyed the opportunity to spend time with his sister.

It was the Valentine Day weekend and this Saturday afternoon was cold and windy. The Sandia's were wrapped in a blanket of clouds with peaks occasionally peeking out of the gray mist as the gusting wind danced about.

There wasn't much activity at the Indian Cultural Center and Joaquina completed her business there in short order. From there they went directly to the Veterinary Outlet to complete their shopping chores. Then using the map Mrs. Savage had given them they proceeded to the University area to search for Alan's apartment. As they were driving down Central, Joaquina saw a window display full of red and white valentines. On impulse she asked Billy to pull over and park. She came out minutes later with a heart shaped box of candy wrapped in red cellophane. She glared at Billy and asked, "Please, don't say a word. I'm trying hard myself to understand what this is all about." She placed her purchase into the grocery bag Mrs. Savage had packed the pies in.

With Joaquina acting as navigator and properly interpreting Mrs. Savage's map, they drove directly to Alan's apartment.

It was Sandy who answered the knock at the door, obviously happy to see them, especially Billy. "Come in this house and be our guests." Then yelling back into the other rooms, "Hey guys, come look what the wind blew in from Zuni"

As Alan entered the room Billy threw the laundry bundle at him saying, "it was a long cold drive just to make sure some ugly mama's boy has clean underwear."

Alan put down the laundry and gave Joaquina a big hug as he reached behind her to take Billy's out-stretched hand in a solid grip.

About this time Will came to see what all the commotion was about and stopped completely in mid stride as he saw Joaquina. There was an awkward moment as everyone in the room seemed to sense the electricity and energy being exchanged by this couple standing quietly, yet obviously communicating; their smiling eyes saying volumes.

Sandy broke the silence, "We were just sending out for pizza and then we're heading for The Pit; the Lobo's are playing Brigham Young tonight and it's an important game in the WAC standings. You may be able to get some SRO tickets and join us."

Joaquina said, "Thanks, Sandy, the pizza sounds great, but I'm no basketball fan. I brought my bedroll and a good book, and I'm chilled to the bone after that long drive in Billy's truck."

Just as Alan was getting ready to add his voice, Sandy interrupted saying, "Leave your bedroll in the truck, you can sleep in my bed and Billy can sleep on the couch."

Alan concurred, "Just what I was about to suggest. I'll sleep easier knowing that Sandy's bed is already full and the ugly Zuni won't need to go sleep-walking."

At this Billy was looking around for something to throw at Alan and lacking that said, "Only and ugly Anglo harboring ugly thoughts would think of such a thing." Then he looked quickly at Sandy to catch her reaction to Alan's comment and his response. Her innocent smile didn't convey any message whatsoever to Billy and that was as she intended.

The pizza was gone and the last of the apple pie was being devoured. Will, who hadn't had much to contribute to the last hours conversation announced, "I guess I won't go to the game after all and this way Billy can use my ticket and the three of you can sit together. Besides, I have a test Monday that I could study for. And I can keep Joaquina company and perhaps she can answer some of the many questions I have." At this announcement all the room were looking at Joaquina to measure her reaction when Will added. "And we won't be needing a chaperone. The snow hasn't begun to melt in the high country."

Joaquina smiled at this. Neither Sandy nor Billy understood the relativeness of a chaperon and the high country melt. Alan had the advantage and said, "And the coyote whelps remain unborn."

Joaquina was the only one present who understood the gravity of these last two utterings, and the thought that two of these fine young men would soon sleep with their ancestors was a sad and frightening knowledge to possess.

It had been some time now since the trio of basketball fans had left for the UNM arena referred to as The Pit. Will came into the living room where Joaquina was curled up on one end of the couch with her book and a blanket.

"May I join the pretty lady?"

"Be my guest, handsome young man," was Joaquina's reply as she put down her book.

The next hour was spent with Joaquina and Will first asking then answering each other's questions. They earnestly endeavored to bridge and close this cultural gap that would deny the attraction they obviously held for one another.

It became an especially educational and interesting evening for this Minnesota lad with his limited knowledge of Native American culture, both past and present.

Joaquina explained, among other things, a study she had been involved in regarding the obesity and diabetes in the genes of Native Americans.

"For example," she said, "Take Sandy, a beautiful woman, yet she probably weighs well over two hundred pounds. Her ancestors were hunters and gatherers and virtually lived with feast or famine. They developed over generations the ability to store fat in their bodies for the lean times. These genes have been passed down from one generation to the other. If you will notice, Sandy probably doesn't eat as much as you and Alan, yet she gains more weight every year, especially if carbohydrates are introduced into her diet. Her metabolism is not designed to burn up the calories you and Alan can. I am very fortunate that I do not have this problem. Grandmother Maria has suggested that several generations back some Spanish genes probably account for this good fortune."

"Diabetes is another burden we carry. The incident of diabetes is greatest in the Native American population and especially within the Zuni populace. Along with our history of myths and religious beliefs, you should also be aware of some of the unwelcome baggage we bring to a relationship."

At this Will took her in his arms and kissed her softly on her cheeks and then passionately on her lips and said, "All I know is that you have moved into my heart and there seems to be no room left for doubt or concern.

Perhaps I'm being naive but surely the old saying that love conquers all cannot be discounted."

Joaquina pushed him gently back and said, "Give me a minute to catch my breath," and left the room.

In a matter of minutes she re-entered the room with nothing but Sandy's Navajo blanket wrapped around her and gave Will the box of Valentine candy saying, "Won't you be my Valentine/" and at the same time taking him by the and leading him into his bedroom.

Will saw lightning cross the sacred mountain, heard the eagle scream on high, and would never ever again see the world as it had been before this night.

Joaquina was also wrapped in an emotional blanket of love that seemed to be at once, sensuous beyond belief, but also holding the specter of death waiting in the shadows.

They lay there for some time, each deep in thought, each totally physically and emotionally exhausted. Will was sound asleep when Joaquina quit his bed and silently returned to Sandy's before the Lobo fans returned.

It was a raucous group that morning as they took turns at the two bathrooms and polished off the mountain of scrambled eggs Sandy had made.

It was no surprise when Sandy announced she was off to mass and invited this band of heathens to join her. Now, both Will and Alan were Protestant but had on numerous occasions joined Sandy at mass. They especially enjoyed the guitar mass at St. Bernadettes and this is where they all went this cold and dreary February morning.

Will and Joaquina sat next to one another, enjoying the closeness and unspoken love that was binding them ever closer.

Will was offering a prayer of thanksgiving for this gift of love he had received, rationalizing that surely a loving and forgiving Father would not judge them harshly for their departure from ordained social mores.

Joaquina, on the other hand was praying as desperate a prayer as she had ever prayed in her life. She was begging God that it would be possible for these three young men to see the aspen turn gold, knowing that her heart would surely break if her new found love were to be taken from her. Yet how could she place him over her own brother or Alan, who had been like a brother these many years?

She was also praying for forgiveness from this her second indiscretion. But how could this be wrong when her entire being was caught up in this all-consuming fire of love and desire. She left the service drained emotionally, full of indecision, full of fear of the future.

It was a long , cold trip back to the Pueblo and Billy sensed something had taken place and allowed her the unasked-for silence. It had been a long and silent ride with only the quiet noise of the wind whistling through the poorly insulated cab of Billy's pick-up. Finally the shadow that was Corn Mountain loomed ahead and the warmth of Grandmother Maria's kitchen welcomed them home.

PUMA

It was mid-February and the promise of spring filled the New Mexico skies. A false promise for sure, for spring-time in the Rockies is always a perfidious program.

Will was up early, studying for an upcoming exam when the phone rang. "Will, is that you? Mr. Savage here, I hope I didn't call too early, but I wanted to catch you before you left for class. I need your help this week-end. All three of you, if possible. We need to move a herd of heifers down to the calving pens, and we've already delayed this chore too long. We're gonna be losing some more calves if we don't get it done. Tell Alan to come up Friday night and we'll get an early start and try to get it done in one day. Billy Otero and the Yazzie's will be here, but we've a lot of ground to cover and it'll take all of us. If I don't hear differently I'll plan on the three of you. Mrs. Savage says hello to you all."

Will's response was quick and positive, You can count on me, Mr. Savage, and I'm sure I can speak for Sandy. I presume Alan's presence is not necessarily a request."

"Dress warm kids! See ya Friday; appreciate it." And with that Mr. Savage rang off.

Friday afternoon Will was the first one back to the apartment and spent his time waiting for Sandy and Alan packing his duffel. He couldn't imagine why they were running so late when he finally heard the pick-up pull into the driveway.

Alan yelled for Will as soon as he entered the room, "Hey Dude, get out here, we've got something for you."

As Will came into the room he saw Sandy standing with something hidden behind her back. As he approached her she said, "Close your eyes and bend down a bit."

As he did so he felt Sandy placing a hat on his head. "Now take a look in the mirror and see if you don't agree it's a great improvement over that feed store gimme hat you been wearin'."

Will couldn't have agreed more, for he was wearing an expensive black Four X Beaver Stetson with a beautiful beaded hat band. It was blocked the same as Alan's without the sweat stains.

Alan added his comments, "Sandy and I decided it was high time you looked like a New Mexican and not a clerk for an implement dealer.

Sandy said, "Don't lose that hat band Will, it's very special. A Lakota lady and friend of mine, Sally Iron Blanket, made it for me."

A stop at Wendy's for a sack of burgers and they were on their way, arriving at the ranch a little before ten, just in time for a piece of Mrs. Savage's pie, still warm from the oven.

While they were all admiring Will's new Stetson, Mr. Savage offered, "I'd wear something with ear flaps in the morning. Howard Morgan on the channel seven weather report is predicting a front moving in from Arizona with a falling glass and probable snow. I'm hopin' we can have the cattle outa the timber and headin' for the pens before it hits. So plan to quit the sheets early and we'll break the fast about five, be saddled and movin' out by six at the latest."

Saturday morning and five o'clock came in a hurry. It seemed to Will he barely got the sheets warm when the alarm went off. Breakfast was spent with Mr. Savage laying out the assignments and plans to accomplish the drive. They were joined at breakfast by Billy Otero and the Yazzie brothers. Billy had arrived late last night and stayed in the bunk house with Jason and Justin.

It was decided Will would go with Billy, Jason with Alan, and Justin and Mr. Savage would team up. Sandy would drive the pick-up with her mare in the back and have the pen gates open and help with the last stages of the drive. Justin and Jason had hauled hay all day yesterday getting the corral ready and repairing some downed fence.

The corrals were flanked on the West and North by a wind break made from pine slabs from the lumber mill in Grants, that no longer operated. The corrals could accommodate well over a hundred head of cattle. A loading chute and crowd pens on the south end completed the design.

At the tack room all but Will picked up their own saddles and gear. Billy picked out the gear for Will. He selected a double cinch modified roping saddle for Will and saddled a docile-looking buckskin mare for him.

Sandy loaded her horse into the pick-up with the stock rack and left the corral in the predawn darkness, heading for the calving pens. .

It was a little before six as they headed west toward

the high pasture and Will thought he may have dressed too warm. It was a rather balmy morning for February and he thought Mr. Morgan's weather report had missed the mark.

Mr. Savage and Justin were in the lead with Billy and Will bringing up the rear. Will was the only one not wearing chaps and spurs. Mr. Savage was wearing bat wing chaps but no spurs. The gelding Mr. Savage was riding had been doing his bidding for years and he allowed as he could communicate with his equine quadruped without inflicting pain. .

Both Mr. Savage and Billy Otero had a rifle scabbard with a thirty thirty for Billy and a thirty aut six for Mr. Savage. The Yazzie boys had cut sign of large cat back in December and Justin had earlier this week found the half-eaten and hidden remains of a freshly-dropped calf. This discovery had added emphasis to the need to move the heifers down to the calving pens. That and the predictable springtime weather with its propensity for wind and snow.

Billy and Will were working the south end of the drive and had been out of the timber for some time now and had a dozen heifers moving easily along in front of them, when all of a sudden Billy reined his horse to a stop, took his rifle from the scabbard, and jumped to the ground all in one swift move. The report from Billy's gun set Will's horse to bucking and he nearly lost his seat but somehow managed to stay aboard. By the time he accomplished this, Billy was back in his saddle and riding hell bent towards a stand of aspen with his rifle still in his hand. Will, leaving the cattle, who had scattered at the sound of the rifle, followed quickly behind.

As he neared the aspen, Billy jerked his horse to a halt, ground tied it, and scanned the aspen looking for the cat he knew he had hit. By now both horses had picked up the scent of the mountain lion and were acting skittish. At this point Will heard one of the most frightening and carnal sounds he had ever heard. The wounded cat screamed a warning that would surely chill the blood of the bravest soul.

Mr. Savage and Justin, working the center of the drive, had heard Billy's shot and now the Puma's mournful cry. Justin, a bit more superstitious about these animals, let out a string of Navajo that Mr. Savage could only guess at.

Billy could just make out the tawny piece of fur crouched low in the dry grass in the shadows of the aspens. He moved in closer for a clearer shot, when the wounded lion leaped from its cover and charged the source of its present pain. It must have been no more than thirty feet from Billy when he pulled the trigger, the bullet entering the right eye and smashing into the brain pan, killing the big cat instantly, while its momentum carried it forward to fall almost at Billy's feet.

Billy had instinctively levered another round into the chamber of his rifle and stood there waiting for the cat to move, at the same time trying not to foul his jeans, for he was shaking like the aspen leaves and had somehow lost his breath.

Through all this, Will had managed to somehow keep his horse under him and felt as if he had had a box seat to one of nature's grandest, yet saddest performance. He understood the need to keep this predator from culling the calf herd, and that in the final analysis, Billy had actually acted in self-defense. But here lay dead one of the most beautiful creatures Will had ever seen in the wild.

Billy had regained his composure and had already begun the task of skinning this beautiful creature. Neither one had said a word and Will watched quietly while Billy completed this chore.

Billy finally broke the silence, "We've got to get back

to the drive and I doubt that horse is gonna stand still for this." With that he took out his bandanna and fashioned a blind-fold over his horse's eyes, and then lifted himself up into the saddle saying, "Now Will, I need you to hand me that pelt while I try to manage this horse."

Will couldn't believe the size and beauty of this hide. Surely it must have measured over nine feet from head to tail. Billy had said it was a big female and probably accounted for keeping more than one deer herd in check.

It was no easy chore to hand up the hide to Billy, who draped it doubled over the front of his saddle and then asked Will to untie the blindfold from his horse. At first the horse seemed to be going to accept this added passenger, but after about five seconds began bucking and crow hopping, managing to dump both Billy and the cat in the sagebrush.

Billy picked himself out of the sage, walked over to his horse and began to tie the reins to the saddle horn, at the same time directing Will, "Here's what we'll do, I'm gonna walk this pelt down to the pens. I'm damn sure not gonna leave it here for the coyotes to drag off. This old horse will stay with yours and you can go back and gather the heifers and keep the gather moving ahead of you ranging back and forth from this south fence to the center where Mr. Savage and Justin are working. Tell them what happened and maybe someone can come back for me."

Will had returned and gathered up the dozen or so, they had moved out of the timber and increased his gather by another dozen. He was feeling very confident and rather proud of what he was doing when he was presented with another challenge. He had just topped a draw where he could look down into an arroyo running north and south and there he could see a heifer, obviously in the last stages of calving.

In the last hour the temperature had dropped more than twenty degrees and the wind had picked up; now it was starting to snow, tiny flakes that were dry and cold and stung like cactus. He had some time ago retrieved his parka from behind his saddle and was wishing he had worn the long underwear Alan had offered him this morning. As he was thinking this he looked at Billy's horse with Billy's coat still tied behind the saddle. It was going to be a cold and maybe dangerous hike Billy was taking with his Puma pelt.

Will sat there on his horse for some time watching the heifer in her labor. Even to his untrained eye it was obvious the young heifer was having trouble disgorging the calf trying so hard to enter this cold and windy world.

After some time, it was becoming more and more obvious that if he didn't intervene they could lose both the heifer and her calf. Trying to apply some basic horse sense to this situation he arrived at a decision, dismounted and taking his pigging string from the saddle he wrapped a quick tie to the little legs protruding from beneath the heifers tail. The he returned to his horse, retrieved his lariat, tied it to the pigging string and the other end to the saddle horn. Now he tried to urge his horse ahead slowly taking up the slack and steadily pulling, and finally successfully bringing this new little life into a snowy, chilly February afternoon.

There wasn't time to go through the proper ritual that calf and mother must perform at this point. Will assisted in the removal of afterbirth, lifted the newborn up onto his saddle and climbed up behind, to continue the drive towards the pens. The new mother, confused by all this, eventually trailed along and followed the horse carrying her calf.

It seemed to Will that the temperature must have dropped another ten degrees and the wind had picked up several knots. The snow was starting to accumulate and was drifting into the draws. He thought he had heard a horn honk earlier and was sure he could see the pens down the valley. He felt he had managed to keep his little herd together and he saw that Billy's horse was still with them.

About this time he sensed a movement to his left and at the same time heard Mr. Savage call out to him.

"Hi, Will, rein up a minute." Will halted his horse and waited for Mr. Savage to ride up along side.

"looks like you picked up a passenger."

Will tried to smile through the cold and replied, "His mother was having trouble and you're looking at a midwife. I couldn't leave him for the coyotes and if you're wondering where Billy is, he shot a lion and skinned it out but the horse wouldn't haul the hide so he's walking it in."

Mr. Savage said, "We heard the shots earlier and figured it was either a lion or coyotes. and I noticed you had Billy's horse with you. Let's move your gather along and join up with Justin. We're lookin' at the pens over the next rise."

Sure enough as they topped the rise Will could see through the blowing snow the pens with the gate open, and Sandy riding out to meet them.

No sooner had they pushed the last heifer through the gate when Mr. Savage asked Will for his horse. He said, "Will, let me have your horse, and you head back in the pick-up with Sandy. This old horse of mine will pack a lion, or a bear, or whatever, with no trouble. I'll go pick up Billy and see you back at the ranch. Make sure Sandy's tally agrees with Jason's or get another count.

Have the boys break some hay bales before they head for the ranch. I'll meet you all back there."

Will helped Sandy load her horse in to the pickup and jumped in behind her, glad he didn't have the long cold ride back to the ranch. The heater in the pick-up was already throwing out some really welcome warmth. What a day this had been! He had watched a mountain lion killed and a calf born.

Sandy said they had corralled no less the sixty-three heifers and of course one calf. Mr. Savage would be pleased and she said he would be glad the threat of lion kills had been taken care of.

It was near dark when Will heard the corral gate open and looked out to see all four riders coming home. Will put on his parka and hurried out to help take care of the horses.

While they sat around Mrs. Savage's dinner table enjoying the efforts of her day's labor, they heard again the exciting tale of the way the lion charged Billy and the accuracy of his shooting under such pressure. There was also some praise for Will at his first attempt at cowboying and calving.

Mrs. Savage understood Will's concern and comments about what a shame it was to see such a beautiful animal killed, and she offered, "Will we make our living with our livestock and we can't afford to feed predators. If they cull the deer herds, that's fine, but when they get to the point where they have to expand their range and add livestock to their diet, something must be done."

"The neighbor hired a trapper last year because the coyote population was getting out of control. They wiped out two flocks of wild turkeys and who knows how many quail and cottontail. I hear he killed about forty coyotes that winter."

The group adjourned to the den and gathered around

the fireplace where the conversation turned to, chiding Billy about his questionable horsemanship and the question of whether the shot through the lions eye was pure luck or because he had his eyes closed.

That night as Will pulled the Navajo blanket up around him and listened to the wind howling outside, he offered up a prayer of thanks for this incredible day and the wonderful world he was living in.

JENNIFER SCANLON

The United flight was running about forty minutes late due to traffic control at Denver. Will rushed from his last class, concerned his sister might be kept waiting. Now all that rushing and concern was for naught. While waiting for the delayed flight, he was enjoying the art that decorated the newly refurbished Albuquerque International Airport. The gate room boasted a Snidow original of some cowhands wearing yellow slickers with reflections of them and their horses in puddles from a recent rain. Will thought Snidow and Morton were two of the best western artists in the Southwest. The beautiful bronze at the end of the concourse by Lincoln Fox was especially appropriate for a Southwest airport.

Finally the flight pulled into the gate and commenced disgorging its passengers. Will began to believe his sister was not on board but eventually she emerged with more carry-on luggage than is allowed.

"Hi, Will, hope you haven't been waiting too long. I had no way of calling you. The Denver traffic is unreal. We waited in a line of at least thirty aircraft waiting to take off." All this while putting down her carry-on luggage and giving her brother a sisterly hug and kiss.

Jennifer Scanlon was an attractive thirty-one years, an accomplished and successful woman. She had earned a Master's degree at UNM and then gone on to Stanford for her Doctorate in Anthropology, and was currently the assistant curator of the Museum of Anthropology in Minneapolis. She was enroute to Chaco Canyon to continue research on a paper she was doing on the Anasazi. She would be spending several weeks in New Mexico, then back to Washington D.C. for a meeting with the Minnesota Congressman regarding continued grant money for this important research.

"How's our mother" asked Will as they gathered up her carry-on luggage and headed for baggage claim

"She's just doing great, Will, and sends her love and orders to increase your level of correspondence. Perhaps you're investing too much free time with social activities. How are your grades?"

"Didn't Mom tell you I made the Dean's list" And, Jennifer, you just look great. When are you gonna get married and make me an uncle?"

Jennifer smiled and answered, "Can't you handle having an old maid for a sister? I still see Mac on occasion and he keeps asking when we're going to get married." Mac McIntosh was an attorney in St. Paul. He and Jennifer had gone to High School together and had been seeing each other for over a year now.

"Well sis, get crackin' and marry that Mick and make me an uncle. I always liked Mac and I understand his law practice is rather lucrative. And face it, Irishmen make wonderful lovers and husbands."

"Here's my luggage. I'm staying across the street at the Amfac. Do they have a courtesy car?" Let me get checked in and then I'll buy you a drink and dinner on my expense account. It'll be a chance to get some of your tax dollars back. We're still working on grant money."

Will and Jennifer had always been close, even with the half dozen years separating them. They were jumping from one topic to the next at a rapid pace trying get caught up on all that had taken place in the past months.

They had opted to have dinner at the Amfac and it was half-way through the first cocktail that Will took Jennifer's hand and asked, "Jenny, how would you like a Zuni Indian for a sister-in-law? Wait'll you meet her. She's the most beautiful and enchanting creature this Land of Enchantment ever produced. And you get to be an instant aunt. She has a two year-old boy who'll tug at your heart strings."

Jennifer was caught off-guard to say the least, but she knew her brother was not an impulsive soul and would not take such a step lightly. He had always been mature for his age. Four years in the Marines and travel all over the world had broadened his horizons considerably. If he had fallen in love with this woman and her child, it was surely more than infatuation or a purely physical response to a beautiful woman. In the past, all of his female companions had been capable of qualifying for the cover of Fifth Avenue. Her handsome brother had never had a problem attracting the opposite sex.

Well into their second cocktail he was still talking a mile a minute, trying to bring Jennifer current on all that had happened in such a short time. He told her about Alan and Sandy and the Savages, and the Diamond G, and the Yazzie brothers, Billy Otero, the Shalako Ceremony, Grandmother Maria, the Puma, his roll as midwife with the calf, and how much he loved New Mexico and had never been happier in his life.

It was obvious to Jennifer that he was, indeed, happy. He fairly radiated happiness; it was almost contagious as he went on about these new-found friends who apparently were considered family. She was anxious to meet them all.

She finally had to interrupt him, if for no other reason than to give him time to eat before his steak got cold. "Will, let's coordinate our calendars. I've got nearly two weeks planned this trip and let's see what all we can crowd into it. How would you like to take an airplane ride tomorrow morning? I've got to call Mueller Aircraft and confirm a charter for tomorrow morning. An engineer from Sandia Labs is coming along with the latest state of the art in infra red camera equipment. We'll be taking photographs of Chaco Canyon and the ancient road network to the outlying Anasazi communities. We'll be looking at the Escalante area west of Delores, Colorado, Chimney Rock in Southwest Colorado, and the outlying Houck and Allentown areas in Arizona."

These outlyer communities were part of the continuing mystery of Chaco Canyon. In 1980 Federal legislation designated thirty-three such sites, all related to the Chacoan culture, many adjacent to the straight line road network. The Chacoan culture reached far beyond the ten-mile-long Canyon of Chaco to a thirty-three thousand square mile San Juan Basin. Jennifer in her continuing quest to solve some of these mysteries was cataloging and recording these outlyer ruins and the road network that tied them to Chaco Canyon.

Will's response was immediate and positive, "Jenny, that sounds fantastic. If you've got room, count me in, and maybe we could fly over the Diamond G I'd love to see it from the air. And next week end how about freeing up your schedule and I'll arrange a trip to the ranch and the reservation. You can meet the Savages and Joaquina, your future sister-in-law, and Joaquin your future nephew, and, of course, Grandmother Maria. Speaking of Grandmother Maria, here's a little something for my favorite sister."

With that he pulled out of his shirt pocket a beautiful Zuni fetish hand carved by Grandmother Maria.

"Oh, Will, it's beautiful. You shouldn't have spent so much, I know what these cost, and a student on a fixed income can't afford to be so generous. But you know how I love Indian jewelry. And knowing it's from Joaquina's grandmother, I'll treasure it even more."

And with that she offered her brother another hug and sisterly kiss.

Early the next morning Will picked Jennifer up in front of the Amfac and headed for the Mueller hangar where the engineer from Sandia, Joe Kitta, was waiting for them with his camera and related equipment.

The weather was more than obliging with not a cloud in the sky. The Mueller pilot helped them aboard and they were quickly aloft and on their way. They headed out east over the Four Hills community then banked left and followed I-40 west toward their destination.

Will especially appreciated the opportunity to fly over the ranch, and they caught Mr. Savage and the Yazzie boys working with the cattle at the calving pens and Mrs. Savage out in the yard hanging up her wash. Wait until they hear it was Will in that low-flying aircraft that tipped its wings and buzzed them. Won't they be surprised!

Joe Kitta surprised both Jennifer and Will when he told them he had taken pictures of the ranch and the buildings and would enlarge them to a colored photo 18 X 24 suitable for framing.

Finally, Will would have a gift to give the Savages. His efforts in the past never seemed to him to be an adequate thanks for all they had done for him.

What a day this had been! They had certainly seen a lot of New Mexico, not to mention, Arizona and Colorado. Jennifer could now begin to understand Will's fascination with New Mexico.

It was long past dark when Will dropped Jennifer off at the Amfac and confirmed plans to pick her up early Saturday morning at the Park Superintendent's office in Chaco Canyon.

EXTENDED FAMILY

Will had quit the sheets in the middle of the night and dressed quickly, not needing to be quiet because Sandy and Alan had left for the ranch last night. He turned onto I-25 and headed for Bernalillo and the road to Farmington.

It was still dark when he turned off the highway and started south on the twenty six miles of poorly-maintained road to the Chaco Canyon park headquarters.

With about ten miles to go on this dusty, rutty road, pock marked with chuck holes that would swallow up a small vehicle, the eastern horizon was showing signs of pink announcing the coming day

When Will pulled up in front of the park headquarters, Jennifer was already out and waiting for him, and the sun was well up now. She had packed an overnight bag and was wearing boots, jeans, and a most beautiful Zuni fetish.

"Turn off your headlights , Will. And where did you get the fedora, Tex?

Will was also wearing levis and boots and his black Stetson.

"This is a gift from my roomies, and I would just as soon be called an S.O.B. as to be called a Texan. How goes the research? Nice fetish."

They continued south on more dirt road, every bit as bad as the twenty-six miles he had just driven. This brought them out a little below Mount Taylor and put them at the ranch mid-morning.

Sandy, Alan, and Mr. and Mrs. Savage were all out front waiting as Will pulled in and parked next to Alan's pick-up.

"Jenny, meet my New Mexico family, Mr. and Mrs. Savage, and my roomies, Sandy Yazzie, and Alan."

Mrs. Savage was the first to speak and offered her hand as she said, "Welcome to the Diamond G, Jennifer. We've heard so much about you from Will, and I must say he's certainly proud of his sister."

One after the other they each made Jennifer welcome; she could see that Will had indeed found an extended family in New Mexico. It was obvious that Will and Alan could be mistaken for brothers. and as Will had described him Mr. Savage was truly a replica of Gary Cooper. Sandy was every bit as beautiful and heavy as Will had described her.

The ranch house was even more charming then Will had described it. they were joined at lunch by Jason and Justin. The lunch Mrs. Savage prepared reflected her love for cooking, as always. She had insisted they stay for dinner and the night. Will told her they had a tight schedule and Joaquina was expecting them for dinner.

They made good time and there was still plenty of daylight left when they saw the Sacred Corn Mountain in the distance. Will had shared with Jennifer his limited knowledge of the Zuni and the events of the Shalako back in December. She had taken advantage of the limited library at Chaco Canyon Park headquarters and invested some of her time in her own research of the Zuni people. With all her research of Anaszai culture over the years, she was a bit of an expert on the Southwest Indian culture past and present.

Joaquina was waiting by the front door when they pulled up and immediately came out to meet them. She waited for Will to initiate any display of affection, not wanting to offend in any way Will's sister. Will went directly to her and took her in his arms and kissed her long and passionately. Then turning to Jennifer, "Jenny, this is Joaquina. Joaquina, this is Jennifer, the other woman in my life."

Joaquina rather timidly held out her hand to Jennifer, who reached beyond the outstretched hand and took Joaquina in her arms and enveloped her in a warm embrace and said, " I'm so pleased to meet you Joaquina. Now I can understand what has happened to my brother. I was sure the woman he has been describing and raving about couldn't possibly exist, but I see she does."

Joaquina was a bit embarrassed and lowered her head slightly in that attitude of timidity and humility that Will found so captivating and becoming. Then she looked up and said, "Welcome to Zuni, Jennifer; I hope we can make your stay with us comfortable."

At this point Grandmother Maria came through the door carrying little Joaquin, who, as she put him down, came running into the outstretched arms of Will, yelling , "ride, ride"

Will scooped him up onto his shoulders, "There ya

go, Skippy, now hang on tight or this bronco will buck you off." After several quick turns around the car he set the lad down, took his duffel and Jennifer's overnight bag and started for the door when Joaquina said, "Will, Jennifer will be staying here but you will be staying over at my aunt's house with Billy."

Will returned his duffel to the car and carried Joaquin into the house.

Billy Otero joined them for dinner, and as usual, Grandmother Maria had outdone herself. With Joaquin's help they had indeed provided Jennifer with a suitable introduction to the truly Southwest cuisine. The blend of Mexican and Indian culinary art made this a memorable feast.

Here again Jennifer could appreciate these people that made the extended family of her brother. There was no doubt he had surrounded himself with a diverse and interesting circle of friends since his arrival in New Mexico.

After dinner, while Billy and Will were busy spoiling Joaquin, and Grandmother Maria was clearing the table, Joaquina asked Jennifer if she would like to walk down to the river.

They were almost to the river before either of them spoke. Joaquina spoke first saying, "What had Will told you about us?"

Jennifer thought about what she was going to say and after a lengthy pause said, "He tells me he has never felt like this before, nor so sudden in his decision to marry. He has never been one to be indecisive nor has he been impulsive. He is always deliberate and thinks through before he acts. He feels you love him as deeply as he loves you, but says there some reluctance on your part he cannot comprehend. Something about snow melting in the high country."

Joaquina had decided early in the evening that she was going to like this sister of Will's. Already, she was sure, they both were feeling comfortable with one another.

"Jennifer, I love your brother beyond measure. I am not naive enough to think that there will not be some cultural canyons that must be bridged. But our love for one another will conquer this. To explain my reluctance it will be necessary for me to share with you a confidence, and place upon you a terrible burden. I have discussed this with Grandmother Maria and she has chosen, for reasons I do not know, not to answer my questions regarding her devastating prediction. Tell me now before I go further, can you promise to keep in absolute confidence that which I am about to share with you?"

Jennifer was both intrigued and frightened. The wind was blowing off the river and the darkness that falls before moonrise made this evening seem darker and colder than Jennifer could ever remember. Being a Minnesota girl she was used to cold, but this was a different kind of cold, almost an inner chill. The cold fear that seemed to embrace them as they stood there on the river-bank was cold and foreboding.

Jennifer felt herself shudder as she said, "Joaquina, you are scaring me. I know this is about Will. You are surely aware by now how much he and I mean to one another. I also know how much the two of you mean to one another. Yes, of course, I will not betray your confidence. But please, Dear God, tell me nothing is going to happen to my brother."

Joaquina reached out and took Jennifer's hands in hers and began to share the terrible burden of Grandmother Maria's prediction. "The first night I met Will, he and my brother Billy and Alan Savage had driven up from Albuquerque to attend the Shalako ceremonies. My Grandmother has been blessed, or cursed, depending on interpretation, with the far seeing-eye. She can see into the future."

"The night they arrived she came out of the kitchen to greet them and apparently saw their future. She cursed in Zuni and ran back into the kitchen. I followed her to find out what had taken place. She told me that of those three handsome young men, two would not live to see the snow melt in the high country and would be gone before the coyote whelps were weaned."

"Now you too must carry this terrible burden. But it is much worse for me. For one is my brother, one is my good friend, and one is my love. I cannot bear the thought of losing any of them and yet I know two of them will not see the aspen turn gold."

Jennifer was nearly in shock. She did not speak for what seemed a long time, and then finally, "What must we do? What can be done?"

Joaquina answered, "Nothing can be done, nothing can be changed. We will wait, that is what we will do, because there is nothing else we can do. We will carry this terrible burden in our hearts and we will pray that we will be able to accept with grace that which will happen. We will pray for strength."

After a long time Jennifer asked, "When will the snow melt in the high country?"

"Mid summer." was Joaquina's reply. "Come my sister, let us return to our loved ones."

THE ICE CAVES

It was Alan who picked up the phone, "Alan es aqui, que pasa?"

It was Jennifer Scanlon on the other end and she replied, "Nada que pasa, Senorita Scanlon es aqui, donde esta me hermano?"

Alan laughed, "Hi, Jennifer, just a minute and I'll get him for you." Then yelling back into the other room, "Will, it's your sister."

"Yeah, Sis, what's doin'?"

"Will, remember when we were flying over the Malpais last week and Joe Kitta pointed out the volcanic cone called Bandera and the story about the Ice Caves? Well, I've been thinking about them and I want to drive over and look see this weekend. How about joining me?"

"Great Sis, just what I need, more reasons to get out

of studying. Okay, but only because it's your last week-end and I won't be seeing you for awhile."

At Will's remark, Jennifer felt the cold fear settling over her like a damp wet rug that she couldn't crawl out from under. She quickly shook off that feeling and responded, "Pick me up early and we can get in our little tour and back to Albuquerque in time to catch my six p.m. flight to Minneapolis."

"Sounds good, Sis, See ya Saturday as the early morning's first rays penetrate the Canyon Chaco, when the ghosts of the Anasazi retreat to their ruins to hide and wait for another moonrise. How's that for pure poetry?"

"You never cease to amaze me Will, I await your limo. Bye, bye."

Once again Will had hit the road early and conquered the twenty-six mile endurance test into Chaco Canyon headquarters, and as before Jennifer was standing outside with her luggage ready to go.

"Did you see any Anasazi ghosts retreating into the ruins, Will?"

Will laughed and replied, "No, and that's because there's no morning's first rays. I drove in fog most of the way. It looks like a cold dreary day for your last bit of New Mexico. But based on the Channel Seven weather report, it's fifty degrees warmer than it is in Minneapolis."

They loaded Jennifer's luggage and headed south as they had before on a rutty washboard road.

The Perpetual Ice Caves are located twenty-six miles southwest of Grants on New Mexico highway number 53, just off county road 129.

The Ice Caves are truly a phenomenon. As far back as 1540, Zuni Indian guides gave Coronado a tour of the Ice Caves. The Candelaria family, the present owners of this unique piece of New Mexico geography, have made it available to tourists for a small fee.

About a mile and a half from the entrance to the Ice Caves is Bandera Crater, volcanic monument. Left over from eons ago, this breached cinder cone rises 450 feet above the lava flow of ages past. Bandera is a Spanish word meaning flag; it refers back to a time when a military expedition planted a flag near the top of the crater's cone.

Summer in the Malpais (Spanish for bad lands) reaches temperatures well over 100 degrees, but just eighty feet or so below the surface the temperature in the Ice Caves remains a constant thirty degrees .

How were the caves formed? How did the ice get there in the first place? What keeps it from melting? These are the questions the tourist ask.

Molten lava solidifies at different rates as it cools, depending upon the thickness of the flow, the temperature of both ground and air, and the precise chemical composition of the lava. If the surface lava cools first, forming a crust, occasionally the flow beneath the crust flows through completely, creating lava "tubes" that may be more than a mile long.

One such tube on the Big Island of Hawaii is over a mile long and will accommodate a full size auto.

As surface water seeps into these "tubes" or caves through cracks in the lava, it meets dense, cold air that is sinking into the cave. The air circulation diminishes as the warmer air rises to escape the cave. The lack of circulation keeps the cave at a constant thirty degrees. The Malpais above the cave also act as an excellent insulating material.

The Malpais are the most recent land set aside by Congress as a wilderness area and consist of 84,000 acres of abrasive basalt lava.

There are many stories of lost treasure in the Malpais. Some of the more famous are the Lost Adams Diggings purported to lie hidden somewhere in the 119 square miles of Malpais basalt.

There are factual records of treasures found in this maze of razor-sharp lava. They include Indian water jugs filled with bones and Spanish coins, and an iron chest filled with $10,000 in Confederate bills. In the middle of all this lava lay the "hole in the wall," 14,000 acre island of grass and trees that was too high for the lava to cover.

Depending on the source, the tales are many and varied of treasure seekers that entered and never returned from a search in the Malpais. Compass readings are false due to the iron in the lava.

Where some tourist would be disappointed with the Ice Caves, Jennifer was intrigued and told Will she had some theories regarding the Anasazi and the Ice Caves and the Malpais. She was more than glad she had taken the time to visit this area before she left.

She thanked Will for the extra curricular activity and the early pick-up, and they commenced the long ride back to Albuquerque to catch her flight.

As her flight climbed over Four Hills and banked left, Jennifer looked out her window at the grandeur of the Sandia's rising up out of the desert floor, and wondered at the magnitude of the events of these last two weeks. The quiet snows of Minnesota would perhaps give her the solitude to sort out and ponder over events that might change her life.

WASHINGTON D.C.

Jennifer had been waiting over twenty minutes now, and the taxi she had requested was nowhere in sight. She had decided to wait another ten minutes then call Mac for a ride to the airport. She could not afford to miss her flight; she had an appointment for lunch with her congressman and her flight was scheduled to arrive at the Dulles Airport at 10:50 a.m. .

Finally, she stepped out to the curb as she recognized the yellow vehicle rounding the corner. As usual, the driver didn't budge from his seat and let her open her own door and place her luggage in the seat beside her. He would probably repeat this scenario at the airport and still expect a tip. Jennifer had decided to herself, "Not a chance, Bucko."

The traffic by now was quite heavy and four inches of new snow was slowing it down considerably. Spring's reluctant arrival was a given in Minnesota. It reminded Jennifer of Will's comment that, "Springtime in the Rockies was the most perfidious program in the world."

Finally arriving at the United Airlines terminal, she had about sixteen minutes to clear security and make it to her gate. And as she had expected, her driver, who had spoken no more than three words the entire ride, remained seated while she unloaded her own luggage. She gave him eighteen dollars against his fare of seventeen sixty, and left the door open as she left. She could hear him grumbling as he went from the warmth of his seat to the cold blowing snow to close the passenger door. She had a moment of remorse as she thought about the smallness of character such action personified. But on second though, perhaps it would serve as a lesson. Wonder of wonders, the flight was pulling into the gate four minutes early. As she was walking off the mobile lounge she saw a young man holding up a sign reading, "Jennifer Scanlon." He introduced himself saying, "Ms. Scanlon, I'm Fred Banks, from Congressman Lindquist's staff. I just dropped off Mr. Mazimoto from the Japanese Trade Delegation, and the Congressman called your office for your flight information so that I could intercept and provide you with ground transportation."

Jennifer was pleasantly surprised, "Thank you, Mr. Banks, how thoughtful of the Congressman. I have no checked baggage so we may proceed directly."

She was thinking to herself, "How thoughtful, I'm here seeking a sixty-thousand dollar grant and I'm getting the red-carpet treatment from a Democratic Congressman, and have never voted their ticket." She was reminded of the saying, she could never remember whether it was Teddy Roosevelt or Hemingway, "If you're not a liberal when you're young, you have no heart, and if you're not a conservative when you're old, you have no brain."

Congressman Larry Lindquist welcomed her with a warm handshake and took her carry-on luggage, placing it behind his desk saying, "I don't mean to rush you but we have a date in the dining room with Congressman Myles Martinez from New Mexico. He is going to co-sponsor our request for the grant.

Congress Martinez was a most handsome young man who was born and raised in Aztec, New Mexico, and was very knowledgeable about Chaco Canyon. His grandfather had taken him to the site when he was nine years old and he had been back on numerous occasions. He had also supported Senator Domenici's efforts to protect the Malpais.

The luncheon turned out to be more than Jennifer could have hoped for. The New Mexico Congressman had certainly done his home-work. He had already drafted requests to submit to NASA for satellite photos of the Canyon's road network and outlier communities. He had also read Jennifer's presentation on the need for digs at two of the outlier sites. Further, he had read the most recent reports on archaeological studies of the Canyon.

The Congressman from New Mexico was also well versed on his Indian constituents and offered this piece of humor to his fellow Congressman.

"The Navajo alphabet has six T's and the inflection placed incorrectly could mean something totally different than intended. For example, the same word means either outhouse or ballot box, depending on the inflection. Rather appropriate, wouldn't you agree?"

As this luncheon meeting was coming to a close, Congressman Martinez asked Jennifer, "If you don't have plans for this afternoon I would like you to join me. I have a two-thirty date at the Smithsonian that I think you will find interesting.

Jennifer was delighted and suggested she check into her hotel then meet him at the appropriate building at two-thirty.

Thanking Congressman Lindquist profusely, she said she would post him the additional information he required, then caught a cab to the hotel.

Checking into the Downtown Sheraton the desk clerk had a message for her. It was from Mac and it was a local number. She called at once.

The secretary with the law firm of Hodges and Brewster answered and put Jennifer on hold while she located Mr. MacIntosh.

"Jenny, thanks for returning my call. I must have caught the flight just behind yours. We're trying to fend off some lengthy litigation for one of our clients and I had just enough time to run home and pack a bag. What's chances for dinner?"

"Oh Mac, how great, I'll look forward to it. How about six-thirty, I'm in room 809."

"Done pretty lady. Should I wear a black tie or is it informal?"

Jennifer was smiling when she answered, "Knowing you, you'll probably want to send out for pizza. Yes, of course dress up, I know a really neat seafood restaurant in the tidal basin with lots of atmosphere to go along with the great food.

"Done again, favorite lady, see you at six-thirty, gotta go do law stuff,. Bye, bye."

Jennifer had been waiting no more than five minutes when Congressman Martinez hailed her as he came up the walk to the Anthropology building.

He introduced her to the gentleman accompanying him, "Ms. Scanlon meet Joseph Ohnway, War Chief of the Zuni Nation. Chief, this is Ms. Scanlon, the Anthropologist doing the Chaco Canyon research."

The Chief had more wrinkles than a piece of sun-dried leather, and his regal bearing reflected the epitome of a royal chieftain. He wore a bright blue head-band, silver and turquoise necklace and bracelets, a velvet shirt, levis and moccasins.

It turned out he was a close personal friend of the Oteros and as a boy, and also in adulthood, sought the healing services of Grandmother Otero. He recalled meeting Jennifer's brother Will and spoke highly of Alan Savage and his parents.

He was there to retrieve, on behalf of the Zuni Nation, an ancient Kachina Mask and skeletal remains unearthed during an archaeological dig in 1937.

Jennifer was a fortunate observer to a religious ceremony by this Zuni Chieftain as he formally accepted these treasured religious artifacts.

After this moving ceremony, Jennifer had an opportunity to visit further with Chief Ohnway. She was full of questions about the mysteries surrounding Chaco Canyon.

The Chief listened politely and told Jennifer, "Not all of the knowledge of the Anasazi is for sharing outside of the tribal members. Some of this ancient knowledge is only passed on to certain families and offices."

She specifically asked for his thoughts about the theories regarding a lost burial site or grave yard.

His response came after an awkward silence, "The Zuni obviously possess a reverence for the dead that many Anglos don't share. I offer as an example the ancestral remains I am retrieving this very day. We are taught from childhood regarding the dead and the consequences of disturbing these spirits. I would suggest to you that pursuit of different artifacts would be as beneficial, without being as offensive."

Jennifer thanked the Chief for permitting her to

observe the ceremony and to convey her regards to the Oteros. She then thanked Congressman Martinez for all his help and thoughtfulness and returned to the hotel to update her paperwork.

It was six twenty-eight when Mac arrived with a small bouquet of spring flowers. "Something pretty for my pretty lady."

"Come into my room, you punctual pilgrim. Let's catch a cocktail in the hotel bar and then we can catch a cab to the restaurant. I think it's very romantic that you chase me half-way across the continent to take me to dinner. I suppose the flowers mean you're going to propose marriage again."

Jennifer was bursting with all the good news this day had brought.

Later in the evening, they did indeed discuss the matrimonial future.

EASTER

It was Good Friday and Sandy had been up before dawn packing for the weekend and making a breakfast treat for Alan and Will. They had wanted to get an early start for the ranch and the start of spring break. Mrs. Savage had invited the Yazzies and Oteros and, of course, Will, to join them for Easter dinner.

Will was especially looking forward to seeing Joaquina again and hoping they could find some time to be alone. He really wanted to discuss seriously the future with Joaquina and perhaps a commitment beyond her "snow melt in the high country," which he was having trouble interpreting and understanding.

He felt he had done well on exams this past week and in high spirits and welcomed the relaxing atmosphere of the ranch.

Sandy's breakfast treat was buckwheat pancakes, eggs,

and bacon, and she didn't want it eaten cold. "Get in here right now, I didn't get up before dawn to serve a cold breakfast."

Alan, just getting of the shower, didn't take time to dress. Throwing on a robe, he crowded past Will, beating him to the table and yelling back, "C'mon ,Will, we don't want that long drive with an empty belly and an angry Indian."

Both Will and Alan gave rave reviews on the breakfast and offered to clean the table and do the dishes. But Sandy knew they hadn't packed and declined the gracious offer. It was not quite seven when they started up the ramp to I-40 and headed west.

Both Mr. and Mrs. Savage were waiting in the front yard when they pulled in. Will was getting to feel more like a member of this family and these frequent reunions always generated a lot of hugging and kissing, something he was surprisingly growing accustomed to.

After unloading their duffels, Sandy turned down the offer to stay for lunch and said she would take Alan's pick-up and drive to the reservation, and meet them in Grants Sunday morning for the Easter Service.

There was a treat in store for Will. After lunch they saddled up and the four of them, including Mrs. Savage, headed up-mountain for a fishing trip to a high country lake that produced trophy cutthroat trout.

A pack horse carrying tents, bed rolls, fishing tackle, cooking gear and groceries had already been packed, and off they went through the pine and into the aspen, heading for timberline.

The weather was cooperating; it was a beautiful warm spring afternoon. During a rest stop to check the pack horse and adjust the cinches, Mrs. Savage said to Will, "What do you think of New Mexico and the Diamond G country by now." His answer was slow and deliberate,

"I think I have landed among the most beautiful country and the most wonder family this side of the Sacred Mountains. I don't know what I have done to deserve it but I am truly grateful and am trying very hard not to take it all for granted."

Mrs. Savage smiled and took Will's arm in hers. They walked arm in arm to the overlook where they had stopped on the ridge. As they looked out over this panorama, stretching away it seemed forever, they stood quietly saying nothing, just enjoying the glory of a spring day, the warmth of the sun, and each other's company.

As they turned to return to the horses, Mrs. Savage affectionately squeezed Will's hand, "You know, Will, you have become a son to us, and we treasure your presence on these visits."

Smiling and wiping a tiny tear from the corner of his eye, Will said, "You have always made me feel like a member of your family, and when I say family, I include Jason, Justin, Sandy, and Billy as well as Alan. You truly have a large and wonderful family and will never be without family about you. I am most grateful to be a part of it."

It was late afternoon when they broke out of the timber to look down on a jade jewel shining in the sunlight. The west shore of the lake was steep granite giving way to a Sandy beach to the south and east. As mountain high country lakes go it was perhaps smaller than most, probably no more than one hundred twenty acres. In the shady areas there was still a reminder of winter with snow and ice; the lake had been ice-bound only two weeks before.

They quickly set about setting up camp, intent on getting in some fishing yet this evening in hopes of fresh fish for supper.

Alan and Mr. Savage were pleasantly surprised at Will's prowess with a fly rod, and the contest began. The fish were ravenous after a winter being ice-bound and all of them were catching and releasing fish at a steady pace, keeping enough for the supper meal and of course the trophies, to win the four dollar pool for the largest fish.

It was Mrs. Savage who came up with the largest fish, as she declined the suggested nymphs Alan had tied and chose instead to use some of the leeches she had harvested from the grass along the shoreline. She always contended that natural bait found in the lake or stream was by far the best. Her theory had merit, as she, more often than not, took the prize for the largest fish.

It was Mr. Savage who prepared the piscatorial delight over a camp-fire with an old iron skillet. He was quite proud of his culinary skills in campfire cuisine. And to top it off he had packed a bottle of Paul Mason Emerald Dry and chilled it in a nearby snow drift.

What a meal, what a grand and glorious day. Alan offered a toast , "Ayer ya es un sueno y manana solamente una vision; pero hoy, bien vivido, hace cada ayer un sueno de felicidad, la vida es buena, gracias a Dios."

Mrs. Savage interpreted if for Will, explaining it was an old Spanish rendition of the original Sanskrit. "Yesterday is already a dream, and tomorrow is only a vision, but today well lived, makes every yesterday a dream of happiness. Life is good, thanks be to God."

Alan added to his toast, "I have enjoyed more love than most and hope one day to bring home a wife that will give you many grandchildren to share in this love."

It was Mr. Savage that said, "Amen to that, son."

It was late Saturday afternoon when they lifted the pole gate at the corral and unloaded and unsaddled the horses. It had been an outing Will would treasure in his bank of memories. Mrs. Savage headed for the house to prepare the fish they had brought down with them, and then to start preparations for the Easter dinner. Including

Will, Alan, the Yazzie boys, Billy, Joaquina, and Sandy, there would be nine of them for dinner tomorrow.

Easter morning dawned clear and sunny. At the breakfast table Mr. Savage commented on such a beautiful Spring day saying, "And the voice of the turtle was heard throughout the land." And they were indeed, as no less than half a dozen turtle-doves adorned the rail fence in the rose garden.

Mrs. Savage always had feed out for the birds and bird book near the kitchen window to determine the proper nomenclature for some of the seasonal visitors. A family of eight quail were daily visitors along with pinion jays, sparrows, robins, juncos, finches, and an occasional curved bill thrasher.

They left the ranch after an early breakfast and headed for Grants and the early service at the United Methodist Church. When they pulled into the parking lot there was Sandy waiting for them, and to Will's surprise, also Billy and Joaquina.

He knew they had both been invited to Easter dinner but didn't expect them to join them for church. This must surely be a part of Sandy's doing. Not only was she always encouraging the relationship between Will and Joaquina, her feelings for Billy were certainly no secret.

Will at once went to Joaquina and keeping a respectable appearance gave her a friendly kiss on the cheek. They all looked and smiled at this attempt at proper decorum, knowing full well the intense feelings between these two.

The good Dr. Grigsby gave a soul-searching message that challenged every one present and ended with the promise of life beyond the grave and victory over death for true believers in Christ the LORD.

The Diamond G entourage took up an entire pew and in the Easter finery were a most handsome group.

Mr. Savage looked down the row with pride, as he considered them all family.

They were an enigmatic and ecumenical group to say the least. Anglo Protestants, Navajo and Zuni with a Catholic background underscored with a foundation of their own Indian religion with its teachings of tribal and clan loyalties. A potpourri of God's clay.

At the close of the service as they were filing out, Dr. Grigsby commented on the growth of the Savage family. He had been their pastor for many years, baptizing both their children and burying their daughter. He and Mr. Savage had been friends a long time and had gone on many fishing trips together, although the pastor always disapproved of the occasional libation Mr. Savage indulged in.

Will rode back with Sandy and Joaquina in Alan's pick-up, and Billy took Will's place in the ride back to the ranch. The close proximity sitting next to Joaquina in church and now the crowded seat in the pick-up was driving Will crazy. When they finally got to the ranch, Will said to Sandy, "We'll be in in a minute, I have some things to discuss with Joaquina." Sandy wasn't out of sight before Will took Joaquina in his arms and spent some of the emotion that had been building up. Joaquina's response was more than warm and they finally came into the house radiating for all to see the burning love and desire they had for one another.

Joaquina joined Mrs. Savage and Sandy in the kitchen while Will was subjected to the sly grins and rolling of the eyes by the male crew assembled in the den. Will was quite sure his face was turning red, and glad the women were not there to witness his discomfort.

In an attempt to change the subject, he directed his comment to the Yazzie boys, "You lads sure missed a great sermon."

An awkward silence followed, as none of them seemed predisposed to let Will off the hook just yet, and they all continued to smile and enjoy a little longer his discomfort.

It was Mr. Savage who broke the silence and appeared to be coming to Will's rescue. "Isn't spring a great time of year, the colts and calves cavorting in the pasture, the geese and ducks pairing up and the song birds building their nests, all responding to nature's dictate to join and multiply."

It was then that Will knew he had not been rescued from this innocent teasing and countered in self defense, "I know three Indians and one ugly Anglo that might just be a little jealous because of their apparent inability to attract the opposite sex."

At this they all laughed, and the friendly teasing was temporarily put aside. For deep down they were all happy about this couple whose happiness seemed to be contagious.

Over a table laden with ham, scalloped and sweet potatoes, red beets, green beans, pasta salad, sourdough and Indian fry bread, pumpkin and cherry pie, Mr. Savage offered a toast to family and a gracious God who had surely blessed this home. Then they all joined hands around the table as Mr. Savage asked the blessing, giving thanks for the bountiful life, asking for the gift of a grateful heart, and thank God for the most precious gift of all, the gift of his son, Christ the LORD. A unison response of "Amen", sounded from all present and Joaquina squeezed Will's hand as they commenced to pass around the table the culinary efforts from Mrs. Savage's kitchen.

It was discussed and decided that Will would return to the Zuni reservation with Billy and Joaquina. Billy had invited Will to go turkey hunting on the reservation; Bill would bring him back Thursday in time to help vaccinate the spring calf crop. There were some side bets going on as to how much turkey hunting Will would get done.

As they crossed the last cattle guard, Will looked back at the Diamond G with the long shadows of late afternoon creeping over the buildings and felt as if he had always been a part of this family and this ranch. With his arm around Joaquina they headed west into the sunset with its warmth streaming through the windshield. What a great Easter this had been! Another fantastic holiday on the Diamond G to store in his warehouse of memories

VIA CON DIOS ALAN

It was the Tuesday after Easter, and Mr. Savage and Alan
had just come in from the barn and were sitting down to
lunch when the phone rang. "Mr. Savage, this is Clancy
at the Branding Iron Bar, hate to bother you with this,
but one of the Yazzie boys is here and he's falling down
drunk. There's already been one fight this morning and
another in the making. Someone oughta come get him."

"Appreciate the call, Clancy, we'll be right in." Then
turning to Alan, "It's Justin, he's at the Branding Iron
and he's drunk and fighting, go bring him home. I'd send
Jason but he won't be back from ditchin' the hay field till
near dark."

Alan swallowed the last of his milk and put his cherry
pie in a napkin as he headed out the door. "I'll have him
home in no time, Dad, not to worry." And to his mother's
request to drive careful, "Not to worry, Mom, I will."

Clancy looked up at the clock above the bar and over at Justin leaning back on one of the chairs along the wall by the pool tables. He seemed quiet for the time being but was having trouble focusing.

At that point Clancy looked up with dread as Deputy Sheriff Eppers walked through the door. Deputy Sheriff Lloyd Eppers was a small man in more ways than stature. He was only about five foot four, slight of build with thinning hair, a thin hawk-like nose perched above an unusually small mouth that was not much more than a straight line. It never seemed to smile but always appeared to be frozen in an ugly sneer.

He had spent eleven years in the army as a cook's helper and was separated with a dishonorable discharge, which he had managed to conceal in all his employment applications. He had fraudulently stated that he had served his time in the military as a military policeman and attained the rank of sergeant first class. He had actually never been more than a corporal.

He had spent the last sixteen years in law enforcement in numerous small communities throughout the western states. The newly-elected county sheriff, Sheriff Ray Ramirez, had inherited Eppers along with all the staff of his predecessor. In this short time he had decided Eppers did not have a suitable character for law enforcement. He was full of insecurity, fear, and hate. With the protection provided by his badge and his gun, he had become a terrible bully.

The Zuni and Navajo were more than familiar with the joy Eppers derived from beating up drunk Indians who couldn't fight back. His modus operandi was to handcuff them with their hands behind their back and then beat them unmercifully, often, with a sap, then claim they had apparently been in a fight before he arrested them.

Eppers approached the bar, "Afternoon, Clancy, all

quiet here in the Branding Iron?" Clancy didn't bother to look up from the glasses he was washing, "Yep, dead quiet."

Eppers strolled slowly back to the pool tables and then seeing Justin slumped in the chair walked up to him and studied him for some time before he reached down and grabbed him by the arm and said, "Let's me and you go outside and get some fresh air." Justin could hardly stand he was so drunk, and Eppers had some trouble keeping him upright as he directed him out the back door and into the alley. As soon as the door closed behind him he pulled out his sap and came down hard on the back of Justin's head. Justin collapsed in a heap and Eppers pulled his arms behind his back and cuffed him. Then he lit a cigarette and waited patiently for Justin to come around so he could begin his little sadistic game.

Justin was beginning to stir and Eppers threw away his second cigarette and helped him to his feet. As soon as Justin was upright, Eppers hit him with all his might in the belly. Justin went down with the wind knocked out of him. He was trying to get air back in his lungs when Eppers gloved fist smashed into his mouth.

Alan came through the door of the Branding Iron looking towards the back for Justin. Not seeing him he asked the bartender if he had seen Justin Yazzie. The bartender looked up and recognized Alan. "Deputy Eppers took him out back, be careful son."

As the door opened Alan saw Eppers drawing back his arm for another punch at Justin's face. Alan yelled, "Hey, what the hell's going on?" As he approached, Eppers jumped back out of the way and Alan knelt down and lifted Justin's head up off the ground. "Oh, Justin, what's he done to you?" And he turned to look up just as Eppers caught him alongside the head with his sap. Alan fell face forward alongside Justin. Eppers' sap had caught him square on his temple. He was dead before he hit the ground. This fine handsome young man, his life just beginning, dead in a dirty back alley behind a bar. And the snow melt in the high country was still months away.

Eppers was near panic. He knew he had killed this young man. All he had intended to do was knock him down but he turned just at the sap came down. He tried to get his thoughts together. He would tell them the Indian did it. That's it ... the drunk Indian got in a lucky punch and killed him.

He ran back inside and yelled to Clancy to call an ambulance, that there had been a fight and one of them was seriously hurt.

Mr. Savage had a premonition and somehow knew when Sarah called him to the house, that they had lost another child. Sarah, dry-eyed but with tears in her voice, relayed the message that Alan had been killed in a fight and Justin was being held in jail on suspicion of murder.

She reached out for him and they held each other so very tightly for a long time, neither saying anything, just holding onto one another. Finally he said, "Call Dr. Grigsby and make arrangements .... I'll go bring Justin home.

Sheriff Ramirez offered sincere condolences to Mr. Savage and said he was sorry to meet him under such circumstances. He began to explain the events of the afternoon and the charges against Justin when Mr. Savage interrupted him, "Sheriff, I didn't come into town on a load of pumpkins, do I look that stupid? I stopped by the Branding Iron before coming over here. I expect to leave here within the next few minutes with Justin Yazzie. I suggest you check with the District Attorney and perhaps have him call me at his convenience. He knows me. And you and I both know Justin did not kill my son."

Earl Savage was an imposing personality in any situation, but here he stood in his sweat-stained Stetson and dirty levis looking down on Sheriff Ramirez, telling him in his soft spoken, deliberate voice just what he expected.

Sheriff Ramirez turned to the desk sergeant and ordered, "Sergeant, bring out Justin Yazzie, find Epper's report and charge sheet and lay it on my desk, then get me the D.A." Turning to Mr. Savage he reached to shake his hand. "Again, I'm truly sorry."

Wednesday morning dawned gray and windy with the threat of rain heavy in the air. Certainly in keeping with the mood that lay like a soggy blanket over the Diamond G. Neither Justin nor Mr. Savage was at the breakfast table and Jason and Mrs. Savage had little conversation between them. They could hear the sound of the pick ax coming from the little cemetery up on the hill above the house. Mr. Savage was digging Alan's grave next to his sister's, and the rocky, hard, still-frozen earth was making this ugly chore even uglier. Both Jason and Mrs. Savage knew he would not want help and that this physical outpouring would burn off some of the pent-up anger at a world in which such a terrible thing could happen.

It was late afternoon when Mr. Savage finally lay down his pick and shovel and returned to the house. As he came into the kitchen, Sarah could see the streaks the tears had left on his dirt-smeared face. He looked at her and tried to smile, "I had forgotten how rocky that ground was." With that he declined her offer of a late lunch, went to the liquor cabinet, poured himself about three fingers of Wild Turkey Rye and drank it neat, then headed for the shower.

Dr. Grigsby stood at the head of the grave. He had finished his eulogy of Alan. He had known Alan since he was seven and had fished with Alan and his father. He had taught at least two different Sunday School classes that Alan had attended along with his confirmation class. He had wanted to officiate at Alan's wedding when the time came. He went on at length sharing some of the things he remembered about Alan, then closed with the surety that they would all be joined together in the here-after, and read the 23rd Psalm.

It was a small group of mourners gathered around this grave site. The Yazzie boys, Sandy, Will, Billy and Joaquina had brought Grandmother Maria at her request. She had always thought Alan was special. Little Joaquin had come along and a few neighbors from nearby ranches. There had been no funeral, just the grave-side service. Will, Billy, the Yazzie boys and two neighbors had been pall-bearers and carried the casket from the hearse to the grave-side.

Little Joaquin looked around and for the first time noticed Alan's absence and asked his Grandmother, "Where's Uncle Alan?" She explained to him in Zuni and pointed to the sky. Will asked Joaquina what her Grandmother had told Joaquin. "She told him his Uncle Alan has gone to live with the cloud people."

Later, as they were lowering the casket into the ground, Little Joaquin said in a voice that all could hear as he pointed to the sky. "Grandmother, I see Uncle Alan in the clouds."

Mr. Savage declined offers to help and began the chore of covering up this hole in the earth that had just swallowed up the still and lifeless body of his son.

Later, when they came into the house to join the group eating from the many dishes of food the neighbors and friends had brought, he called the men into the den. There they gathered around the welcome warmth of the fireplace on this dreary day as he offered this advice. "First, I want to thank you all for being here today to help lay Alan to rest. Now there's some other things we need to lay to rest. I want no thoughts of revenge over this killing. Hate is a cancer and it will eat you up. Walk away from this thing. What goes around comes around, and you pay for every trespass on another soul, if not in this life, then in the next. Nothing we can do will bring Alan back. Let's all hold him in our memories and our hearts." Looking around the room and into each face he finally said, "We're all still family and we all need one another." Then he went to Will and took his hand and said, "Will, Sarah and I will be needing your help from time to time, especially, to get us through the holidays. Don't be a stranger, hear."

Mrs. Savage came into the den, came over to Will and took his hand in hers and said, "Will Scanlon, you were such a friend to Alan. You were both about the same size, I want you to take whatever you want of Alan's things and then give the rest to Good Will. If there's anything Sandy wants, let her have it. I only want the belt buckle Alan won for bareback riding. Bring it next time you come to the ranch. Sandy will be keeping Alan's pick-up and we'll be taking care of the paper-work on that. I imagine you and she will be heading back tomorrow or the next day. Don't be a stranger, Will, and bring Joaquina anytime. You really do make a handsome couple, you know."

The ride back to Albuquerque seemed longer than ever. Sandy was driving and the conversation was limited. They had agreed, however, to make the trip to the ranch as often as their schedules would permit.

THE AVENGER

The Guardian, the local newspaper, had minimal coverage about the death of Alan. On page six it mentioned that Alan Savage had been killed in an accident, that he had graduated from GHS, was attending UNM, and was survived by his parents. Lincoln Favor, the Publisher of the Guardian had been a close friend of Earl Savage for over forty years and had killed the story his reporter had written on the incident. Likewise the District Attorney in concert with the Sheriff had agreed to investigate in depth this unfortunate incident and at the request of Mr. Savage had released young Justin without any charges.

In this same issue on the front page was a story about the discovery of human remains found in a shallow grave behind the Rodeo grounds. An investigation determined the remains were a young Navajo, Paul Begay, who was last seen in a drunken state at the Branding Iron Bar several weeks ago.

Dr. Gerald Montoya while performing the autopsy concluded that Begay had been intoxicated and was obviously beaten to death. Among the findings were broken ribs, a broken jaw, a ruptured spleen and kidney, broken nose, and fractured skull. Upon completion of this autopsy Dr. Montoya began a search of his files, recalling a similar incident. He found it in the autopsy of a young Zuni by the name of Phillip Armijo. It had taken place back in January and an intoxicated Indian had been literally beaten to death.

The strange commonality in these two cases he had failed to note in the autopsy report. He decided to add a post script to the files and cross reference these two files and alert Sheriff Ramirez about his findings. This commonality was the strange imprint on numerous parts of the body, a similar design or pattern. There had been one such mark on the Savage boy.

It was several weeks later when the Dr.'s wife purchased a birthday gift for their teen-age son that he recognized this design. She had brought home a Justin Brand western belt with a popular design called the basket weave. It was often used on saddles, bridles, and western belts. It was also used on wallets, quirts, and yes, even saps.

It had been several weeks since Alan's death and burial when Jason approached Mr. Savage and asked for Friday off so he could take care of some personal business on the reservation. Mr. Savage had intended to move some of the cattle up to the high pastures this Friday and had intended to get Billy Otero to help. Now he would be short handed but it would be a great reason to call Will Scanlon and ask him to come for the weekend. If it turned out Will couldn't make the trip, it would be good for Sarah to get out.

He granted Jason's request and put a call through to Albuquerque for Will. "Will, this is Earl Savage, if you don't have plans this weekend, we need another hand to drive some cattle up to the high pastures. We would start early Friday morning."

Will's answer was immediate and positive, "I'm flattered that you consider my equestrian ability adequate enough to be considered a hand. I'll leave right after class Thursday and be there in time for supper;."

"Billy Otero will be joining us and perhaps you could get Joaquina to drive him down. And ask Sandy to come along, the girls can sleep in the house and you and Billy can share the bunk house with Jason and Justin."

Thursday afternoon classes might just have well been missed for all Will got out of them. He couldn't get his mind off the fact that Joaquina would be sitting next to him at dinner this evening. Finally, the last class was over and he and Sandy were heading west on I-40 about ten miles an hour over the speed limit.

As they crossed the last cattle guard and headed for the ranch house both Mr. & Mrs. Savage came out of the house to meet them, obviously anxious for their arrival. There was the usual hugging and kissing and hand shaking that was part and parcel of arrivals and departures on the Diamond G. On this occasion the absence of Alan was felt by all.

Mrs. Savage noticed immediately that Will was wearing a belt that had been a favorite of Alan's. She at once commented, "Oh Will, I'm so pleased you are making use of Alan's things. I know he would have been pleased. I know I am. I am so glad you took my offer seriously."

Will smiled and replied, "I've certainly upgraded my western wardrobe."

At this point a horn honking and a cloud of dust heralded the arrival of Billy Otero's yellow pick-up. He was out of the door and another round of hugging and kissing and hand shaking began. This outward demonstration is completely foreign to the culture of these Native Americans, but an accepted ritual as part of the Savage extended family. Joaquina joined in this exercise and welcome from Will took an extended and exaggerated duration. All present took delight in watching this young couple so obviously and totally oblivious to the presence of others.

A loud backfire from Billy's pick-up brought them back to the present. It had been dieseling all this time, coughing and sputtering, long after Billy had turned off the key. Billy commented with a laugh, "The old Amarillo Bruja just wants to keep on ticking and ticking."

It was great to sit at Sarah's table and after the first few moments of uncomfortable conversation, Sarah put them all at ease when she offered, "I so hope we will continue to gather as family. Now that Alan is gone we truly need your presence from time to time to remind us of our Alan. He will be in our hearts and thoughts every day and we will miss him especially on these occasions. But it is the wonderful memories and his wonderful friends that will sustain us and make his absence bearable. Please say you will continue to come and grace our table and our home."

After dinner, Sandy suggested to Joaquina that she and Mrs. Savage could handle the clean up and perhaps Joaquina and Will could spend some time together.

Joaquina thought this a grand idea and taking Will by the hand led him outside and they walked arm in arm towards the corrals. Will, after a fashion, directed the conversation to the obvious seriousness of this relationship and asked, "Joaquina, where is this headed? Please tell me that you feel as I do and that we have a future together, and please don't confuse me with talk about coyote whelps and snow in the high country."

Jason was up early Friday morning and out of the bunkhouse before the others were stirring. He intended to make the reservation by mid-morning. The Ramah Navajo Reservation is located Southeast of Ramah, New Mexico. Ramah is a Mormon community dating back to 1876. The Ramah Navajo Reservation consists of 47,000 acres in a parcel of land about 18 miles wide by 30 miles long. The average elevation is 7,000 feet, with the highest points reaching over 9,000 feet. There are deep canyons in the north, while most of the reservation consists of broad valleys of grass and sagebrush bordered by stands of Pinion and Juniper.

Jason was enroute this morning to call upon his Grandfather, Hosteen Ben Joe Yazzie. His grandfather's father had survived the attack in Canyon de Chelly by Kit Carson and was among those who fled and remained hidden for years existing with nothing more than sheer grit and determination, leaving a proud heritage for this clan.

The hogan of Hosteen Ben Joe was located far back in a remote canyon that offered a hidden spring. Jason's grandfather was a healer and singer and performed numerous religious ceremonies. Jason was calling upon his grandfather this morning to ask him to perform the Enemies Way Ceremony.

The sun had broken over the canyon wall some time ago and the valley was bathed in bright sunlight. Jason could see a wisp of smoke coming from the hogan. He pulled his pick-up along side a pinion arbor and leaned against the fender waiting for some time, allowing those inside to recognize their visitor and in their own good time deciding whether to acknowledge that presence or not.

After some time Hosteen Ben Joe opened the door of the hogan and stepped out into the bright sun. Shading his eyes with his hand he looked for some time at his visitor.

Jason spoke to him in Navajo, "Good morning, Grandfather, this is Jason, your grandson,"

The old man had more wrinkles than a dried prune and appeared older than he actually was. He wore his white hair in the traditional bun and sported a faded red head band. An old blue shirt and faded levis along with the traditional moccasins completed the costume. A squash blossom necklace and turquoise bracelets on each wrist were the old pawn jewelry. Incongruous to this was the white leather belt with a buckle depicting a pair of crossed golf clubs.

Jason and his grandfather sat for most of the morning under the pinion arbor and discussed many things, all in Navajo. It was determined that his grandfather could not perform the ceremony he requested within the time frame Jason required. It was decided Jason would return at a later time for a purification ceremony. Jason spent the rest of the day and that night with his grandfather, leaving after breakfast the next morning.

It was almost noon Saturday when Jason walked into the Branding Iron Bar and took a seat in the back near the pool tables. He recognized several Navajo he knew and was offered a drink. Jason had never touched alcohol and never intended to. He had seen too often the terrible results of this poison and continued to practice, for the most part, the teachings of the Navajo Way. After some time he satisfied his thirst with a soft drink and continued his attention to the arrivals coming through the front door. He was almost caught off guard. It was nearly four in the afternoon when he caught through the corner of his eye the opening of the back door and the arrival of Deputy Eppers. He immediately slouched in his seat and assumed the appearance of a drunken passed-out Indian.

Eppers walked from the rear of the room to the front looking over the situation and strutting in his arrogant manner with his hand resting on his revolver. Returning to the rear of the bar he watched a pool game in progress for awhile when he saw Jason slumped in the chair. He made several trips up and down in front of the apparent drunken Indian when he finally reached down and shook his shoulder. Jason mumble almost incoherently, "Go away."

Eppers reached down and took him by the arm and lifted him out of the chair saying, "let's go outside and get you some fresh air, fella." Jason continued his act, falling and leaning heavily on the short little bellicona that was propelling him through the back door and into the alley. As Eppers was reaching for his handcuffs, Jason brought his high-heeled boots down hard on Eppers instep, at the same time pivoting with his elbow, catching Eppers in the throat. Eppers was bent over gasping for breath when Jason kicked him in the belly. It was a kick that would have made a Denver Bronco punter proud. Before Eppers could fall to the ground Jason brought his knee up into his face breaking his nose and several teeth. As Eppers finally fell to the ground his revolver fell out of it's holster and as he reached for it the heel of Jason's boot broke numerous bones in the scrawny little hand. Jason pulled him to his feet and planted his fist one more time into the ugly little face. Eppers collapsed unconscious to the ground.

It had all happened so fast, Jason wasn't even out of breath. He had gone about this ugly chore with an almost disinterested business-like attitude. But he wasn't finished. He reached into his pocket and took out his pocket knife. A three bladed Boker Tree Brand made of Solingen steel and razor sharp. He carved out to V notches on Eppers left ear and one on his right, then picked him up and threw him into the trash dumpster, breaking several ribs as he did so. Taking out his bandanna he picked up Eppers revolver and chucked it in a nearby trash can, then walked up the alley toward the parking lot where he had left his pick-up. It would be necessary now to go through the purification ceremony he had discussed with Hosteen Ben Joe.

The next issue of the Guardian covered on the front page the mysterious assault on the local deputy and detailed the results of this beating along with the strange cutting of the ears.

It was Tuesday of the next week and Mr. Savage and Jason and Justin had unloaded the last bales of hay off the truck when Mr. Savage addressed Jason, "Jason, I understand that every Navajo on the Ramah Reservation knows the Yazzie boys brand their sheep with two V notches on the left ear and one on the right. . Is that right?"

Jason just stared at his boots and Justin offered, "What are big brothers for?

THE INVESTIGATION

Soon after Mr. Savage left his office that fateful afternoon, Sheriff Ramirez paid a visit to the Branding Iron Bar. He questioned the bartender at length regarding the time frame of events that led up to the death of the Savage boy. He stepped out back and surveyed the scene of the incident. He noticed several cigarette butts of the brand that Eppers smoked. Satisfied he had gathered all the information he could find, he headed back to his office to go over the arrest report Eppers had filled out and to spend some time going over Eppers' personnel file.

In the arrest report Epper's had filled out, he stated he had taken the drunken subject out back for some fresh air and the subject had passed out. He said he was waiting for the subject to come around when he heard a commotion down the alley and went to investigate. When he returned he found the Anglo on the ground and the subject had regained consciousness. He then handcuffed the subject and called an ambulance. He did not explain further his investigation of the commotion down the alley.

The personnel file of Deputy Eppers, among other things, contained two annual evaluations and a six-months probation evaluation. All three reflecting, at best, mediocre performance in no less than twelve areas of job measurement.

There were two letters and one in-house note regarding complaints of unnecessary force and abuse during arrests. One of these letters was accompanied by a hospital report detailing the results of a beating administered to an inmate, along with an investigation which was unable to determine when the beating had taken place. Eppers report, attached to the investigation paper-work, stated the subject was in that condition when arrested. The only proof to the contrary was the statement of the subject, and the investigation was dropped.

Sheriff Ramirez was a deliberate, if plodding type, and several days later he again took out Eppers' personnel file. This time he studied in detail the resume it contained, and called in his secretary.

"Send a letter to all the previous employment positions in this resume and ask for a copy of Eppers' personnel file from each. And this is to be confidential. Also get a hold of Agent Keifer at the FBI and tell him I need a favor. I want him to get Eppers' military records for me muy pronto."

Surprisingly enough, the first response was from the FBI. They had the information faxed from the bureau in D.C. . Agent Keifer hand delivered it to Sheriff Ramirez with the offer to assist in any further investigation of Eppers. He said that on two occasions he had received complaints about the deputy's mistreatment of drunken

Indians. These complaints had been passed on by the Indian officers on the Ramah Navajo Reservation.

Ramirez spent the better part of a day going over the file of one Corporal Eppers, cook's helper, who had been separated with a dishonorable discharge.

The information contained in the Army 201 file and the information regarding military service in his resume were certainly not in concert. In fact it was almost as if it were describing two different individuals.

One reported incident that drew Ramirez' attention was a lengthy report about a staff sergeant who received second degree burns in a shower. According to one PFC John H. Riley, "I went to the latrine and saw Corporal Eppers standing at the door to the showers and he was laughing to himself and wasn't aware anyone else was there. When I went to see what was so funny I saw Sergeant Meiers laying on the floor at the rear of the showers. There were three showers turned high on hot and through the steam I could see the Sergeant looked like a boiled lobster. I immediately turned off the showers and ran to the orderly room to call an ambulance. Corporal Eppers was not there when I ran to the orderly room." Riley recalled further that Eppers' shoes and pants were soaking wet.

There were several other depositions accompanying this report, one from PFC Wm. Harvy who had heard an argument and threats take place between Eppers and Sergeant Meiers, and one from a PFC Harold McCormick stating he had seen Sergeant Meiers so drunk he could hardly stand up; this at about the time the shower incident took place. The report concluded that for lack of evidence no charges were brought against Corporal Eppers.

There was another lengthy documented report about a severe beating of a black private, Clarence W.

Washington, who had been tied to a support column in the motor pool garage and beaten severely with the broken handle of a push broom. Private Washington was drunk at the time and could not describe his assailant. Eppers, according to motor pool records, had returned a jeep and trailer with field stoves about the time the beating took place. Again no witnesses observed the actual beating and no charges were brought.

Within the week several more responses arrived in the Sheriff's office/ The Sheriff's office at Morcroft, Wyoming, had never heard of Eppers and neither had the Sheriff from Johnson City, Texas. Both had been listed on Eppers' resume.

Sheriff Ramirez sent out a request through the State Law Enforcement Cooperative Association for any information or record of employment for a Lloyd Eppers.

The first response came from the Chief of Police in Douglas, Wyoming, in the form of a phone call. He described in detail two incidents regarding patrolman Eppers. One involved a complaint brought by parents of a sixteen year-old girl Eppers had grabbed and twisted her wrist when he was issuing a speeding ticket. He threatened to cuff her and take her to jail.

The second incident involved a drunk white male Eppers had arrested and placed in a jail cell. As the drunk began to sober up he promised Eppers he would get even for the beating he had been given. Eppers, either in fear or anger, fired a tear gas shell into the cell. By the time the jailer on duty got the man out of the cell to the hospital, he had lost the sight in one eye. The man sued the city and Eppers. The city settled out of court for three quarters of a million dollars and Eppers left in the middle of the night without a forwarding address and a pending arrest warrant. The Douglas Chief followed his commentary with the statement that their District Attorney would be sending a request for extradition along with the outstanding warrant and asked Ramirez to arrest and hold Eppers.

Lloyd Eppers had been raised on a farm just outside of Council Bluffs, Iowa. His father, a lazy and rather poor farmer, was a mean drunk and when in this condition had beaten young Eppers all but senseless on several occasions. One day when Eppers was about seventeen his father had beaten him with a buggy whip during one of his benders. Later that day Eppers found his father passed out in the barn and tied him up with a strand of baling wire and beat him near to death with a rake handle Then he packed his few meager belongings, stole twenty dollars from his mother's purse, and the family car, and headed for Texas. After bumming around for several months he lied about his age and joined the army. Always a loner and a misfit, he carried his total outrage at drunks to an extreme that bordered on psychotic.

The record of his Courts Martial and dishonorable discharge were detailed and lengthy. He apparently had stolen and sold two jeeps to a Mexican national that the Mexican authorities had been watching for some time. He was easily convinced he should testify against Eppers. Eppers had served four years in Levenworth prison.

Ramirez locked the files away in his desk and would put a call through to the District Attorney when he returned from his scheduled training in D.C.

GATHERING **OF NATIONS**

Billy yelled back into the house, "Get crackin', Joaquina, you're gonna make me late for work." With that Joaquina came through the door with little Joaquin in her arms and handed him to Billy and returned to retrieve the rest of the luggage. Grandmother Maria came carrying her own, which appeared even more ancient then herself. It was an old canvas bag with leather straps that were as wrinkled as Grandmother but seemed more than adequate for the few belongings she packed inside.

Joaquina and Grandmother Maria were dropping Billy off at the ranch and then driving his old pick-up to Albuquerque to attend the Gathering of Nations, the annual Indian Pow Wow with tribes from all over, including some from as far away as South America. There would be thousands of Native Americans from every corner of this land bringing their contribution of dress, dances, and arts and crafts to this great gathering. This year it was to be held at the "Pit", the University of New Mexico athletic arena.

Grandmother Maria was not totally in concert with all the events at the Pow Wow as she remained steadfast in her traditional concepts regarding the ceremonies that related in any way to their religion. She did, however, enjoy the carnival atmosphere and all the colorful dress and delighted in all the native tongues being spoken. She had always espoused the need to retain the way of life handed down through generations that set them apart and made them different from other peoples. She was especially adamant about retaining the language.

The sun was just breaking over the eastern horizon as they pulled onto the highway and headed directly into it. Billy, in the absence of a sun visor long ago lost, pulled his sweat-stained and battered Stetson low over his squinting eyes and almost appeared to be sleeping. The drive to the ranch was quiet with the exception of little Joaquin asking now and again about the rabbits, refer-ring to the road kill the ravens and magpies were making their breakfast.

As they crossed the last cattle guard and started down the fenced lane to the house, Billy could see Mr. Savage and Jason coming up from the corrals and Mrs. Savage coming out of the front door. He couldn't remember a time when he arrived at this home that he wasn't greeted in the front yard. As Billy's old yellow pick—up pulled to a stop and disgorged it's passengers, the usual unIndian hugging and kissing took place.

Sarah gave Joaquina a hug and a kiss as she took Joaquin in her arms and smothered him with the affec-tion a grandmother would, then reaching out with a free hand grabbed Billy and pulled him close enough for an affectionate kiss on the cheek. Out of respect and an understanding of her wishes, they settled for just a handshake with Grandmother Maria. Mr. Savage threw a quick handshake at Billy and gave Joaquina a warm hug as he invited them for breakfast. He had just assumed that Sarah would have prepared something and he was right as the smell of cinnamon and fresh bread led their way to the kitchen.

When Billy mentioned earlier in the week that Joaquina and Grandmother Maria were going to the Pow Wow, Mrs. Savage had suggested, no...make that insisted, that she take care of Joaquin until they returned.

After breakfast Billy and Jason left to join Justin who had left earlier with the backhoe. They were building a series of check dams in the high pasture. Mr. Savage took Joaquina by the arm and walked her to the front door and asked her to deliver a message to Will. "Ask Will to call me if he doesn't have classes or a job lined up this summer. I need a good hand to summer range the cattle on the BLM lease up on the divide. The pay is good and he'd have some solitude and an opportunity to study. Tell him we wouldn't leave him alone up there all summer and that we'd send Billy or Jason up there to spell him now and again."

Mr. Savage had been running cattle on this government land through a lease with the Bureau of Land Management for over twenty years. It was located on the continental divide and would accommodate between fifty and sixty head of cows. About ten years ago they had built a line shack and pole corral to replace the sheep-herder's tent and hobbles they had always used.

Joaquina had made the horseback trip into the line camp last summer to deliver supplies and clean laundry to Billy, and was familiar with the setting. The line shack was set on the edge of a stand of Aspen which looked out over a rather pretty lake that gave way to a vista to the north that reached out to include the sacred mountain of the Navajos the Anglos called Mount Taylor and the Sandia and Monzanos on the distant eastern horizon. She replied with enthusiasm, " If I can't convince him this is an opportunity most would kill for, I'll apply for the job myself." At this Mr. Savage laughed, knowing that she could indeed handle the job as well or better than most men.

As they stepped outside Joaquina, glancing at the back of Billy's pick-up exclaimed with alarm, "Our luggage, it's gone." Thinking the worst, she feared they had either left it back at the reservation or it had fallen out enroute.

Mr. Savage was quick to allay her concern, "Not to worry, Joaquina, I had Billy put them in the trunk of the Buick. It's all gassed and ready to go. There's no way Sarah would let you try to make it to Albuquerque in Billy's old pick-up. Besides we haven't put enough miles on that car to justify havin' it on the place.

As Joaquina adjusted the seat so she could reach the pedals and Grandmother Maria tried to figure out the seat belts, Sarah held Joaquin up to the window for one last good-bye. He didn't seem at all concerned that his grandmother and mother were driving off without him. It was Sarah who was still waving as they crossed the last cattle guard and pulled out onto the highway. Joaquin could hardly wait to get to the corrals. Sarah had promised him he could ride one of horses.

Joaquina was enjoying the luxury of the ride in the Buick and the usual quiet presence of Grandmother Maria. Quite often Joaquina reflected on the strong feelings that went clear back to her early childhood when she was in the presence of her grandmother. This wonderful old woman radiated an inner piece and serenity that had

always seemed contagious to Joaquina. As she was growing up, her grandmother had taught her many lessons
and perhaps most important among these was the lesson
of the need for moments of quiet meditation and reflec-
tion. She looked at her grandmother who was taking in
the scenery as they sped along I-40 and wondered what
she thought of this fancy luxury car and the four-lane
highway with all its traffic.

Joaquina was feeling proud of herself as she managed
the directions Billy had given her and drove directly to
Will's house. As she wheeled the Buick into the driveway,
both Sandy and Will came out to meet them. They had
skipped their afternoon classes in order to accommodate
their house guests. No sooner had Joaquina stepped out
of the car Will had her in his arms and with respect to
Grandmother Maria's presence, settled for an almost
brotherly kiss. Grandmother Maria pretended not to see
this display of affection and busied herself in conversation with Sandy. Will retrieved the luggage from the
trunk and followed them into the house. Joaquina would
share Sandy's room and Grandmother Maria would sleep
in what had been Alan's room, now vacant.

At the first opportunity, Joaquina said, "Will, if you
haven't made plans for classes this summer, Mr. Savage
wants you to work the cattle at the line camp. It's the
most beautiful spot and he really needs your help and I
could bring up supplies and clean laundry on occasion."
As she said this she looked at Grandmother Maria trying to determine her reaction remembering the constant
ever present burden of the fateful prediction. For the
coyote whelps had long since been born and the spring
run off was commencing. Surely her heart would not
lead her into a relationship of such a short duration. But
the alternative was not acceptable either.

Sandy interrupted this awkward pause in the conversation with the encouraging comment, "Oh yes, Will, what an opportunity! I have been to the line camp and Joaquina is right, it's a beautiful spot and a chance to repay Mr. & Mrs. Savage for all they have done."

Will couldn't help but reflect on all the wonderful doors that had been opened for him since that chance meeting with Alan at registration. His entire life had changed at that point and it seemed all predestined.

Will was quick to respond, "My only reluctance is that I may not be enough of a cowboy to take proper care of his cows, but I'll welcome the chance to finally do something for them because they have done so much for me ... and I'll really look forward to the delivery of clean laundry." It was settled then, he would call Mr. Savage this evening and confirm it and mark the calendar accordingly.

Grandmother had decided she would stay at the house and rest while they went to the arena to register Joaquina for the Pow Wow and find out the schedule of events. Joaquina would be one of the dancers from the Zuni reservation but had decided not to enter any of the individual dances or contests.

Will was not prepared for what he was seeing. He knew there would be several different tribes represented and he would see all kinds of different costumes but he had no idea what to expect. While Joaquina was registering and getting the schedule of events, Sandy was pointing out some of the different tribes she recognized in attendance. Some Will had never even heard of, Gros Ventre, Nez Pierce, Shoshone, and many others. Sandy pointed out a handsome young Seminole wearing a multi-colored shirt. Then she directed his attention to a young woman dressed in white doeskin with beautiful bead work, obviously from one of the plains tribes.

After the registration Joaquina joined them and

introduced them to her friends, Freida Walking Bird and her husband, Charlie Crushed Ice, who were Oglala Sioux from the Pine Ridge reservation in South Dakota. Joaquina had met Freida at the Pow Wow two years ago and they had become good friends and had corresponded ever since. Frieda was a graduate from the University of Nebraska with a BS degree and was teaching seventh grade at the reservation school. Charlie was back at C.S.U. in Fort Collins, Colorado in his last year of veterinary school. They had a young daughter, Laughing Bird, who was a contestant in the junior individual dances.

It was finally time to leave and pick up Grandmother Maria as Will had offered to take them all out to dinner, but he was really looking forward to tomorrow, for today had certainly whetted his appetite. It was only natural that with his chosen profession of archaeology he would find the gathering of so many diverse costumes and cultures exciting and educational.

Grandma seemed rested and happy they were going out for dinner. Will had decided on the La Placita restaurant just off the plaza in Olde Towne. He liked the ambiance of the old Casa Armijo with its three-foot thick walls, tile floors, and its wealth of history. It was also an art gallery in its own right with every wall covered with beautiful and original fine art from some of the Southwest's finest artists.

The Armijo House was built about 1880. According to legend, the old walnut staircase just off to the right as you enter the restaurant was built especially so Armijo's daughter Teresa would have a staircase to descend to show off her wedding gown. A small room was constructed at the top of the staircase to provide some semblance of utilitarian need other than just a staircase going nowhere. There is also a story told by employees about the ghost of a young lady that is often seen on the staircase.

The Mexican food on the menu of the La Placita is some of the finest in Albuquerque and there was not much time spent in deciding what each wanted. Will ordered a carafe of house wine with the intention of a toast and when the time came he asked them to raise their glasses.

With a tear in his eye as well as his voice he offered, "to our departed friend Alan Savage who brought us all together." The three Native American women at his table joined his toast and returned their untouched wine glasses to the table where they would remain so. Will realized too late he had made a faux pas but his teetotal friends had handled it nicely with a minimum of embarrassment and the presence of Alan was felt among them. Joaquina reached under the table and squeezed Will's hand reassuringly.

Will had a rather restless and sleepless night. Feeling the nearness of Joaquina and knowing he would not be with her this night was almost unbearable but dawn finally arrived and there she was fixing his breakfast and as beautiful as ever.

The gathering of Nations was much more that Will expected. The pageantry, the color, the music, the dancing, the blending of the different cultures, the diversity of the tribes, the very number of the tribes represented was almost more than he could take in.

The grand march or entry parade was a veritable rainbow of colors and costumes. It seemed to Will they must have plucked feathers from every bird in the world and sewed them on the different costumes. The painted faces and hair styles reflected the wildest of imaginations. The bells, the rattles, the drums, the prayer sticks, pipes, lances, Buffalo and Wolf heads, feathered head dresses and war bonnets that trailed to the floor, blankets with every color and design imaginable. He didn't think he had ever seen such a spectacular gathering.

He enjoyed the drum and singing contest, and it was all enhanced with Sandy's running commentary and explanation of what was taking place. Joaquina's friend Frieda Walking Bird was terribly proud when their daughter won second in her junior division dance contest.

When it came time for the women from the Zuni Pueblo to dance, Will caught his breath when he spotted Joaquina as the women entered the arena in their traditional dress. He loved her so much he felt his heart would surely burst. She had to be the most beautiful woman in this entire arena. As they entered they commenced their subtle dance steps. Their black dresses has a hem trimmed with a woven border of colorful and intricate design with a woven sash of similar material and design. Each wore a necklace reflecting the Zuni fetishes they are famous for and silver and turquoise rings and earrings representing a small fortune in jewelry. the soft white doeskin knee high leggings over the white moccasins completed the costume. Will was convinced Joaquina was the best dressed woman there... or in Albuquerque... hellfire, why not make it the entire Southwest.

Sandy continued Will's education of this Native American extravaganza, "Now you should know that all tribes and Indians do not approve or participate in the Gathering of Nations. Right here in New Mexico the Jemez Pueblo does not approve of nor participate in this pageant. The Jemez is perhaps the most traditionally conservative of the nineteen Pueblos. The apex of their population circa 1680 was estimated at 30,000. They were one of the largest and strongest of all the tribes in the Southwest. It was the Spaniard Espejo and Franciscan Fathers with their program of succumb to the cross or to the sword that decimated this population along with introduced disease, and by 1720 the population had declined to 325 souls. The 1990 census stated 2,864 Jemez people existed.

"The Jemez feel that the dances are for the most part religious in nature and there is no place for them in the carnival atmosphere represented in the Pow Wows. They find it especially offensive to put numbers on ones back during the dance contests. Surely to be defined as sacrilegious. The Jemez feel that these participants are pseudo-traditionalists and only want to observe tradition on an infrequent basis. The Jemez call these people the, 'wannabe tribe' because they -want to be- traditionalist but only on occasion."

Will was pleasantly surprised by this sharing of lore and current evaluation by Sandy and he thanked her.

She said, "I must hasten to add that the Native Americans that participate in these annual gatherings justify it on the following grounds. It tends to involve the younger people and keeps them interested in their traditional ways and culture and language. It is a great social gathering and bolsters the pride of being a Native American.

All too soon it was over and Joaquina and Grandmother Maria were heading back to the Diamond G and the Zuni Pueblo, and Will and Sandy were heading back to their classes, but Will had reinforced his love for Joaquina and these fascinating people he had come know.

THE GRAVE ROBBERS

Will heard Sandy's voice through that deep sleep that occurs in the morning just as it's time to wake. "Will, hurry up, it's Jennifer. She's calling from the airport in Minneapolis, they've called her flight for boarding."

Will jumped out of bed in the altogether and reached for his Levis, still not quite awake, then realizing Sandy was still standing in the open doorway of his room. He offered a quick apology as he headed for the phone, "Sorry, Sandy, hope I didn't shatter your image of Apollo." Then picking up the phone, "Sis, Will here."

"Sorry I got you out of bed but I waited as long as I could and they just called my flight for boarding. I'm enroute to Albuquerque on the new Northwest Airlines nonstop, sure beats connecting in Denver or Chicago. I got a call last night from Barbara Schlothauer, the liaison for Federal Grants at UNM. There has been some looting at the outllier site we had surveyed in preparation for our dig scheduled for next month. Apparently there was considerable damage along with the looting and we may have to move to another site. If you can break away from class this afternoon, why don't you plan to meet me in her office; it's in the Administration Building. There's the final boarding announcement, gotta run. By hon."

Will hung up the phone and smiled at Sandy who offered, "The conversation I heard on this end consisted of at least three words. It's not like you to let a woman do all the talking."

"Jennifer has always been the wordy one and not the world's greatest listener, especially when she's talking to her baby brother. She's flying in for a meeting at the University and wants me to meet her at the Administration Building this afternoon. I guess there's been some looting at a dig site they were scheduling for a dig."

Sandy shook her head sadly and replied, "The robbing of graves is the worst kind of stealing because it desecrates holy ground and I have seen first-hand the damage these greedy ones commit. When I was just a little girl my grandmother showed me a burial site in a canyon where we were herding our sheep. It had been robbed and the bones and broken pots were scattered on the desert floor. She was very uncomfortable whenever we went near this canyon. There are strong feelings and ancient teachings regarding respect for the dead."

Will arrived at the Administration Building and asked for directions to Barbara Schlothauer's office. "Down this hall and the third door on your left, they're expecting you."

The door was open and as Will entered the office he immediately became privy to some unexpected entertainment in progress. A very attractive woman he guessed to be Barbara Schlothauer, was doing a credible imitation of a lizard. She had somehow transformed her face and eyes to resemble that of a lizard and her tongue was darting in and out to the point that it actually didn't require much imagination to guess she was imitating a lizard.

At this point she noticed her audience had increased by one handsome young man she took to be Jennifer's brother, and absolutely nonplused she reached out her hand and said, "You must be Will, I'm Barb Schlothauer."

Will was shaking hands with a very attractive lady with dark hair and brown eyes that definitely were shining. Her features where very fine but not to the point of fragility and he guessed her at about five four and quickly noticed that all the curves were in the precise amount in the right places. Her handshake was strong and friendly and he thought to himself... if he wasn't so deeply involved with Joaquina he would like to give this one a go. He was surprised to learn later that she had three sons and a husband who had a dental practice. She just didn't look old enough to have a family that size.

When Will came back to the present and managed a, "Howdy, yep, I'm Will." Then moving over to Jennifer, he gave a brotherly hug and kiss, "Hi Sis, always good to see you. sorry about the circumstances."

Barbara introduced him to the other man in the room, "Will, this is Bill Whatley, tribal archaeologist for the Jemez Pueblo. He's the one that notified us of the looting that has taken place at the outlier dig site." Bill reached out and took Will's extended hand saying, "Pleased to meet you. I understand you're going to be an archaeologist . I think that's great. If you follow in the footsteps of your father and sister you can look forward to a very rewarding future. Bill was only about seven or eight years older than Will. He had light brown hair about shoulder length that complemented a well-trimmed mustache with a chiva on the lower lip. With piercing deep blue eyes, a complexion that spoke of wind and sun, he probably weighed one eighty on a frame about five eleven. He was wearing levis and boots and a shirt decorated with a bolo tie.

At this point Jennifer pointed out an extra chair to Will and said, "Please join us, Will. Bill was just getting ready to share with us the report on the damage and you came just in time to catch Barbara's rendition of the local fauna." At this they all laughed again and Barbara seemed to enjoy the fact that her face-making had provided a little levity before they began the discussion about the terrible crime that must be addressed.

Bill Whatley was born and raised on a ranch north of the Bookcliffs which lay just to the north of Grand Junction, Colorado. He attended Fort Lewis College at Gunnison, Colorado, and received his degree in Archaeology from the University of New Mexico. He spent some time with the National Geographic and Smithsonian. He has his own archaeological company and is the tribal archaeologist for the Jemez Pueblo. He was introduced to archaeology at an early age as there were numerous ancient ruins on the ranch and he played among them when he was a boy growing up. As he grew older he sensed the presence of the Anasazi and the stories and history that lay buried in the dust of centuries past. He is one of the fortunate few whose chosen occupation is also a source of joy and fulfillment. These strong feelings were quite obvious as he shared with them his personal knowledge of looting and grave robbing.

Bill commenced his dissertation, "Let me share with you some ugly facts and figures regarding this despicable depredation of hallowed ground. There are more than four hundred thousand recorded archaeological sites on federal land, and New Mexico and the other three states making up the Four Corners Area probably have the majority. New Mexico, Arizona, Southern Utah, and Colorado were home to the Anasazi. Hohokam, Mogollon, Sinagua, and Salado peoples from 200 to 1300 a.d. Archaeological warehouses such as Chaco Canyon, Canyon De Chelly, Mesa Verde, Saguaro National Monument, and many, many others have been plundered and looted by thieves and robbers since they were first discovered, and the present activity has reached almost unbelievable intensity. This disgusting enterprise has increased on the Navajo Reservation by 1,000% in the last decade. Tribal sources believe there are approximately two archaeological sites per square mile in this area. Government records indicate that 90% of all the sites in the Four Corners areas have been robbed and vandalized. New Mexico native and now Secretary of the Interior, Manuel Lujan, has recently directed land-management agencies to focus more attention to policing the 950 million acres owned or administered by the federal government. New Mexico's senator Pete Domenici said the Archaeological Resources Protection Act passed in the 1970's 'was a breach of faith by the federal government.' An amendment passed in 1988 called for stiffer penalties for looters and grave robbers. But this has failed to work also, due to the lack of adequate enforcement officers. Even joint efforts by Forest Service, FBI and local law enforcement have failed to stop this growing illegal enterprise.

Wealthy private collectors make this looting worth the effort and risk. A bowl in good condition taken from the hands of a mummified corpse may bring as much as $10,000 while the mummy itself could bring anywhere from three to five times that price. And the location of this looting is so far back in unpeopled areas that the chance of being discovered is remote and the sad commentary is that even if apprehended the chance of a successful prosecution is also remote. It's the collectors and legitimate galleries that provide the monetary fuel for this fire. One scam is for a collector to buy an artifact from an illegal source for say several thousand dollars and then donate it to a museum with and estimated value of between one and two hundred thousand dollars, thereby creating an inflated tax write-off, eventually costing the tax payers.

Currently, Congress has drafted an amendment to the American Indian Religious Freedom Act that will give Native Americans more involvement in the administration of sacred sites on federal land. The concern of the Native American population over these growing depredations has created a growth of organizations to fight back, e.g. the Medicine Wheel Coalition for Sacred Sites of North America and the American Indian Ritual Object Repatriation Foundation, to name a few.

It seems that these thieves have certainly done their home-work. They study archaeological reports, subscribe to related periodicals, watch survey crews in the field preparing site maps for legitimate digs and move in and skim the goodies before the actual dig begins. Some of these grave robbers are second and third generations. I happened on a site where a backhoe had torn up well over an acre of what was once a sacred burial ground. There were bones and pottery shards scattered over the entire area. It was probably one of the most disgusting sights I've ever seen. The persons who did this had to have had a ghoul mentality, and these same persons are offended by bird droppings allowed to accumulate on their mother's tombstone."

Bill went on to explain that the vandalism to the outlier site must have taken place within hours of the departure of the survey crew because when one of the crew returned the next afternoon to look for a missing tripod he discovered the crime. It was so extensive that a worthwhile dig was out of the question and they were gathered this afternoon to select an alternative site.

After the meeting Will invited Jennifer to join him and Sandy for dinner but she declined as she was planning on returning on the six thirty flight. She told Will she would be back in about thirty days to begin the dig and she would be in touch. Will had indeed spent a most interesting afternoon.

LINE CAMP

Will and Sandy had spent the last three days packing and moving out of the rental house and cleaning up the inside and outside. They had decided to keep it for next fall and were successful in subletting it for the summer. A couple from Cheyenne taking post graduate courses this summer were delighted to find such nice accommodations so close to campus. It would work out well for everybody. Sandy had moved back to the reservation for the summer and Will had stored most of his gear in the garage and would spend his summer working for Mr. Savage at the high country line camp and baby-sitting about sixty head of registered Herefords.

Will had been justifiably proud of his three point eight gradepoint average this first year at UNM. He had worked hard and it would have been an exciting and wonderful year had it not been for the sudden and terrible death of his good friend Alan. Such a waste it seemed and so unexplainable and Will thought, perhaps too often, of Alan who had given him another family and changed his life. Had it not been for Alan he would never have met Joaquina and he could not imagine his world without Joaquina in it. It would be tantamount to a morning without a sunrise or an evening without a sunset; a sky no longer blue but a world of gray with the sameness of days each more dreary than the other.

His thoughts quickly turned to Joaquina for he would leave this morning for three days at Zuni before reporting to the Diamond G for this summer of cowboying in the high country. He took one last look about the house, left a note for the Cheyenne couple about the swamp cooler and the trash pickup, picked up his duffel and headed for I-40 and the Zuni Pueblo.

Although it hadn't been that long since the Gathering of the Nations, he had really missed Joaquina and was anxious to spend some time alone with her.

It was early afternoon when he could see the sacred Corn Mountain looming in the mid-day sun and it was as if he could actually feel the closeness and presence of Joaquina. In his hurry he drove a little faster than he should and had to brake rather sharply as he pulled into the yard in front of Joaquina's house, sending up a cloud of dust to settle on everything about.

Joaquina burst through the door and they were in each other's arms as Grandmother Maria turned and retreated back into the kitchen, not wanting be a witness to this open display of affection. She would never get used to these young people carrying on so in public, things that were so private in nature.

"Joaquina, how I have missed you and I swear you have grown even more beautiful these past weeks. Tell me you missed me, too. God in Heaven, I do love you so."

"Don't blaspheme, Will Scanlon, of course I missed you and you must surely be aware by now of my feelings for you. How could there possibly be any doubt in your mind when you measure the depth of my giving."

At this point little Joaquin had joined them in the yard and Will scooped him up and tossed him high above his head to catch him and hug him to Joaquin's delight and insistence to keep it up.

"More, Will, more." Then quickly changing his attention, as two year olds are apt to do, "Come see, Will, come see my wagon."

His Uncle Billy had made him a wagon with a wooden box and some discarded wheels he had found and a pull rope instead of a wagon tongue. A rather crude effort, but in Joaquin's eyes it was a royal coach. Will pulled him around the yard stirring up more dust to settle on Joaquin and the wagon. Joaquina, seeing the film of dust turning that little head of black to a dusty brown, put a stop to this boisterous fun and picked him out of his royal coach and carried him into the house, assuring him that Will was coming in also, and proceeded to the kitchen where Grandmother Maria was waiting with a wet washcloth to attack that film of dust covering her grandson.

Will retrieved his duffel and threw it next to the couch as he followed them into the kitchen and offered his salutation to the matriarch of this home.

"Good to see you again, Grandmother Maria, I hope you are well."

Grandmother Maria, without looking up from her efforts to reach all the dust on a squirming bundle of worms she was holding, replied, "It is also good to see you, Will. Joaquina tells me you have done well at school and your grades earned you honors. We are proud of you."

Will looked over at Joaquina to measure her response to these words from Grandmother Maria. Will was caught completely off guard for he had never really determined exactly how Grandmother Maria felt about this Anglo that had come into their life. These were the most words and the warmest in content she had spoken to him since he had first met her. Finally recovering from this unsuspected compliment he managed to say, "Why, thank you, Grandmother Maria, yes, I made the Dean's honor roll, but so did many other students."

At this she put little Joaquin down on the floor and he immediately ran over to jump into Will's arms. Then looking directly into Will's eyes, she said, " Yes, but those other students are not calling on my granddaughter and do not have such obvious love for my grandson."

At this Joaquina beamed, for she had so wanted Grandmother Maria to accept Will and the fact that she in effect was, if not encouraging, at least endorsing to some degree this relationship, would surely mean Will would survive her fateful prediction. But if that were the case, what was the portent for her brother whom she loved so dearly? What a terrible burden for her grandmother to carry with this gift God had given her, and she was wishing with all her heart that this terrible prognostication had never been shared with her.

She recalled that fateful night when she first met Will Scanlon, when Grandmother Maria upon entering the room cried out and retreated to the kitchen and later in near tears shared with Joaquina that horrible message, (those three fine young men, two of them will never live to see the snow melt in the high country, they will be gone before the coyote whelps have been weaned.) Those three fine young men were Will Scanlon, Alan

Savage and her brother Billy. And already poor Alan had died at such a young age, under rather strange and bizarre circumstance. She quickly tossed out these ugly thoughts and decided to accentuate the positive for the present and that meant her grandmother who was ultra conservative in passing out compliments of any kind must surely like this young man with whom she had fallen so deeply in love.

After an exhausted two-year-old had been put down for his afternoon nap, Joaquina invited Will for a walk down to the river. The warmth of the afternoon sun and the soothing sound of the rushing stream and the touch of Joaquina's hand sent Will's emotions soaring. As he gazed upon her dark beauty and felt the softness of her skin he was all but consumed by a desire nearly beyond his control.

Joaquina, sensing this and feeling, herself, the heat of desire building and racing toward the inevitable, pushed back from his embrace and in an emotional sob, "No, Will, we must not continue this. We both know where this is heading and we must remember where we are and who we are. I promise you I will come to you at the line camp when Billy is to bring your supplies and we will have two full days together. Just the two of us, and you will come to know me as no one ever has or ever will. I love you, Will Scanlon, I love you as I would never have believed possible. Come, let's go back before we make Grandmother Maria more uncomfortable than she already is."

Two days later, Will reluctantly took his leave and headed for the Diamond G. He would cherish the memory of these last few days spent with Joaquina and her son and Grandmother Maria. He had especially enjoyed the conversations with Grandmother Maria and the little pieces of legend and tribal lore she had shared with him. There had been some truly fascinating stories told by this unread, illiterate old woman who could take her audience on vicarious trips into history with such accurate knowledge and detail you felt as if you were actually witnessing it as it happened. As they sat of an evening listening to these wonderful stories, even little Joaquin was totally absorbed and seemed to understand every word his grandmother uttered. Will had come to love this family and was looking forward to the day he would become part of it.

As he crossed the last cattle guard, he expected, and was not disappointed, to see Mr. Savage heading up from the corral and Mrs. Savage coming out of the house. Was there ever a car that pulled into the yard that didn't get this welcome? Perhaps the sound of a car passing over the cattle guard carried all the way to the house. In any event the welcoming party was always there.

Obviously, Mrs. Savage had been in the kitchen as she was wiping her hands on her apron. It seemed to Will that the handshake from Mr. Savage was stronger and the hug and kiss from Mrs. Savage was longer and radiated more warmth than ever before. He sensed that he may be reflecting for them the aura of Alan and if that was the case he was more than glad, for he had in fact become a member of this family also. Lately he had been continually aware of these many blessings, of being loved and included in these two households, and he tried desperately not to take them for granted and worked at being thankful on a daily basis.

Mrs. Savage was the first to speak, "Welcome, again to the Diamond G, Will, we have looked forward to your coming and I have just taken a cherry pie out of the oven. Honey, get Will's duffel and join us for a sliver of that pie while it's still warm."

After a pleasant quarter hour in the kitchen with

the wonderful smells that always seemed to permeate this room, Mr. Savage said to Will, "Let's go down to the barn. Jason's putting the stock racks on the truck so we can move some horses up to the line camp for you. Justin is up there now. We hauled up sixty head of white faces last Tuesday, and Sarah and Jason helped us drive them up on top. Day after tomorrow we'll take you up there and bring Justin back and you can settle in. We'll send Billy up in two weeks time with some supplies and, meanwhile, if there's any problem, you can make it down to the Johnson ranch and use their phone. Old man Johnson is an old friend and it's his stock pens we use to load and unload the stock and we start the drive from his place. This evening after supper I'll get out the topo map and point out the boundaries of our lease and what I'll expect from a Minnesota cowboy. I think it'll be a great summer for you, Will. I always enjoyed the days spent at line camp. It's really beautiful up there on the continental divide and it's really a pretty easy job if things go right but it demands some long days and a herder's attention to the stock."

The next day was spent trying to cram a life-time of knowledge about livestock and tack and terrain into Will's Minnesota mind. Jason took turns with Mr. Savage sharing all kinds of experiences and do's and don'ts that could possibly happen at a line camp. Jason suggested that he relieve Will so Will could come down and help with the first cutting of hay and learn what it is really like to be a ranch hand. Sensing he was being made sport of, he respectfully declined, which brought a laugh from Mr. Savage, who said, "Wise decision, Will, puttin' up hay ain't the most desirable chore on the ranch."

The day finally came. Right after an early breakfast and another hug and kiss from Mrs. Savage, Jason and Mr. Savage, with Will helping loaded four horses and supplies into the stock truck and headed south for the Johnson ranch. Mr. Johnson came out to meet them as the truck was backing into the loading chute. He was a short, bow-legged little man with a barrel chest, a Stetson that must have surely been a hundred years old with old dry cracked boots to match. His levis must have been at least a thirty-five-inch length on a man with a twenty-seven-inch inseam, for he had rolled them into a cuff that almost reached his knees. His face was wrinkled and weather-worn but as he spit out what was left of some leaf tobacco his smile was warm and friendly.

"Howdy, neighbor, howdy, Jason, this the dude gonna baby-sit them cows this summer?"

Mr. Savage introduced Will to Mr. Johnson. The old man Johnson had a hand shake that was as warm as his smile.

"Young feller, you got any problems up there on the divide you just point your horse down hill and he'll bring you to my back door." With that he reached into his back pocket and took out a sack of Beech Nut leaf tobacco and offered it around before stuffing a large wad in his mouth. He would be chewing alone.

They saddled three of the horses and loaded the pannards on the pack horse and headed up mountain. It was about three hours later when the terrain leveled out and Will could look back down the valley and eastward toward the Malpais and beyond. He could see the cone of Bandera of in the distance. What a panorama! They continued around a bend and sensed they were no longer going up hill but had started a gradual downslope. A meadow opened up in front of them just as they quit the timber. Looking across the meadow they saw a small lake at the south end whose shoreline ran almost into a stand of Aspen, and back no more than fifty or sixty yards from the lake's edge was the line shack with the nearby corral. There were two horses in the corral, indicating that Justin was here and waiting for them. A small string of smoke was coming out of the chimney, and Will was sure he could smell coffee clear across the lake. As they followed the trail around the lake Will noticed what appeared to be trout break the water and he immediately regretted he had forgotten to bring any fishing tackle. But not to worry, he was to find out later there were several rods and sufficient tackle in the shack.

The line shack was utilitarian at best and would not win any architectural awards. Mr Savage and Alan had built it years ago and it had weathered many a winter since. Jason set about moving the horses into the corral, and Justin came out to welcome them.

"Howdy, boss, howdy Will, come on in. The pots on. The stock settled in just fine, Mr. Savage, been no problems atall."

The shack consisted of one long room in a building about twenty by twelve made of notched timber with mud chinked between the logs. One door, three windows without screens, a wood cook stove near the door, two double bunk beds, and in the middle of the room the most incongruous addition, a chrome dinette set. It was setting in the middle of the room seeming to separate what was the bedroom from the kitchen. Hanging over this yellow and chrome table and chairs was a Coleman lantern. The only wall decoration was an old faded calendar showing a scantily clad, well endowed lady and the bold letters, Skelly Oil Co, for the month of February 1967.

Will looked around at what was to be his home this summer and as sparse and as bare as it was he felt somehow warm and comfortable and he couldn't account for the feeling that he knew this is where he was supposed to be at this particular time. It was a strange feeling and it was almost as if it were deja vu.

The four of them devoured the sandwiches Mrs. Savage had packed them. Mr. Savage took Will on a quick orientation tour of the lease and the livestock and pointed out to Will's surprise a belled cow that was the undisputed leader of this herd. How they knew which cow to bell was always a mystery to Will, but at this stage of his apprenticeship there were many mysteries. He knew that as soon as they all left he would think of a dozen questions to ask.

And that time came sooner than Will would have liked. They left Will with two horses in the corral and all the supplies they had packed in, and with a nod and a wave they started back down the trail. They needed to get back to the Diamond G for the evening chores.

They were barely out of sight before Will sensed the quiet loneliness that would be his companion for the rest of the summer. He set about putting the groceries on the shelves and finding just the right place to store his few belongings. He had brought at lest a dozen books and went about setting them on a shelf with the best of intentions of turning every page before summer's end. This done he saddled up the roan mare and took a lengthy tour of his domain feeling like a titled Don surveying his huge land grant. Coming back from his silly day dreams he attempted to count his charges, covering considerable ground and searching in and out of aspen groves and scrub oak, he could never come up with magic number of fifty-six cows. What if he had actually lost two head already? The shadows were getting longer and the temperature was dropping. He would worry about that tomorrow. Right now he was thinking about which can of soup to open for supper.

Will lost track of time and couldn't believe how busy

he was just keeping an eye on the herd. On several occasions he had had to move them back away from the Forest Service fence on the south end of the lease. One day had moved into the other and the only reason he thought Billy should be coming one of these days was the obvious depletion of his larder.

One morning he heard the horses in the corral making noises and acting nervous. He looked across the lake and coming out of the timber was a lone rider. He was coming fast and Will wondered was there trouble of some kind. As the rider came closer he saw that long dark hair flying in the wind and he almost swallowed his heart as he ran down the trail to meet her. She nearly rode him down as she brought her horse to a stop and, leaping out of the saddle, ran to him with open arms. He was out of breath and she was smothering him with kisses till he could hardly catch his breath.

Will didn't know how long they had been in this attitude before the rude interruption of Billy's "That's enough you two, save some for when I'm gone back down the mountain."

Billy had ridden up to them with pack horses laden with the supplies Will was looking for. Joaquina had driven Billy's old pick-up and followed Billy driving the stock truck, and then borrowed a horse from Mr. Johnson. Billy would be going back within the hour and Joaquina would stay the two days she had promised. She could stay no more than that as Grandmother Maria had been left alone with little Joaquin.

Billy was almost embarrassed at their obvious hurry to help off-load the supplies and get him started back down the mountain. He hadn't reached the end of the lake before they headed for the shack, hand in hand.

Once again lightning crossed the sacred mountain and the eagle screamed on high. God in all his glory and wisdom created in his creatures a love that is on occasion so deep and abiding it cannot be explained, let alone described with man's limited choice of words.

The next two days were bliss beyond measure for this couple so in tune with one another, so in love with each other. They did indeed become as one. Halcyon days spent in the summer sun and along the lake, and afternoons spent on the divide enjoying not only unsurpassed scenery but absolute privacy that they continually took advantage of, sharing their insatiable appetite for each another.

All too soon it was over and Joaquina saddled up the Johnson horse and headed back down mountain. Just before she headed into the timber and began the down slope she pulled her horse to a stop, looked back toward the line shack and waved. Will took off his Stetson and waved it back and forth over his head. He couldn't believe he had spent four years in the Marines and here he was with tears in his eyes and a lump in throat that was nearly choking him. He had no idea love could be so terrifying.

THE DEADLY DISCOVERY

It had been over a week since Joaquina had headed back down the mountain, and the loneliness Will felt was like a sodden, rain-soaked blanket he could not seem to shed. He possessed a hunger for her that was all-consuming and caused an ache that encompassed his entire being. Consequently he had been putting in long hours going from sunup to sunset riding herd on the livestock, mending fence, repairing check dams, patching the roof, shoring up the corral and keeping as busy as possible. But to no avail. His every waking thought would somehow return to the beauty of this Indian girl who had taken total and absolute possession of his heart.

He had checked the calendar for the third time this morning and he was sure Billy Otero would be here this day. He was bringing up supplies and was going to stay for several days, and according to Joaquina, was going to give Will a lesson in high country lake fishing.

It was mid-afternoon when Will finally noticed movement in the timber north of the lake. Eventually he could make out the horse and rider and the trailing pack horse. He saddled up and rode out to meet Billy.

"Howdy, cowpoke, got some room in that shack for some more groceries?" was Billy's salutation.

Will's response behind a giant grin was, "I got room for groceries and a bunk for the ugliest Zuni this side of the Sacred Mountain."

Billy laughed and as he did so unwrapped the dally on his saddle horn and handed the lead rope from the pack horse to Will. "Here, take this stubborn critter off my hands before I shoot her. I come near turnin' her loose a dozen times between here and the truck. If it hadn't been I packed my fishin' rod and binocs in the pannards she'd be headin' back to the truck right now and you'd be without your groceries. I'll bet that Navajo is still laughing. It was Jason that picked out and loaded that balky mare in the truck and told me she was broke to lead. I think I just did some of his horse work for him and broke her to lead on the way up here."

Billy always seemed to find humor in almost every situation and had that deep-throated, easy chuckle that was usually contagious. He often seemed older than his years and maintained a philosophical approach to both the mundane and the monumental. For no more formal education than he had, he could discuss at length the most complicated of subjects and was extremely well-read. He was always abreast of current affairs, state, nation and world. He and Will had become the best of friends and would obviously, in the not too distant future, become great brothers-in-law.

As soon as the horses had been turned loose in the

corral and the supplies off-loaded and stored in the shack, Will poured them each a cup of coffee and immediately directed the conversation in the direction of Joaquina, eventually asking Billy how he felt about this situation between him and Joaquina, and what was Grandmother Maria's position.

Billy got up from the table, moved to the door of the shack and spent several minutes looking at the beautiful scenery spread out before them. Then turning with a serious, almost stern look about him, responded to the question. "Well, I can live with Joaquina marrying an Anglo and little Joaquin getting a step-father that so obviously cares for him, but I'm having a real hard time tryin' to understand why such a good-lookin' woman would choose such a butt-ugly sucker as you."

Will had been growing more and more uncomfortable as Billy delayed his response, then even more so as he heard the words 'real hard time tryin' to understand', but let out a long held breath and relaxed as Billy finished his barb.

Billy went on to say, "you have certainly made a favorable impression on Grandmother Maria. Either that or Joaquina has painted you ten times taller than you actually are. You know how conservative Grandmother Maria is and how traditional, and she's in no real hurry to see the Zuni bloodlines diluted and the old ways traded for new. But she's also a realist and knows that love can reach beyond culture and race and if strong and enduring can overcome these differences. I'm not so sure she will be as understanding when I tell her I plan to marry that overweight Navajo girl. But there's some drawbacks there that have delayed this decision. I can't quite accept the idea of having Jason and Justin as brothers-in-law." This brought a round of extended laughter and returned the conversation to the lighter side.

When they finished their coffee, Billy went to his saddle-bag and took out a package wrapped in soft white doeskin and motioned to Will to follow him. Will followed Billy out into the sunlight and up the hill behind the line shack. When they reached the crest of the little hill and Billy was satisfied that the breeze blowing down off the peaks was sufficient, he stopped and handed the package to Will and said, "This is a gift from Joaquina, and I'd say that tree over there looks just about right. I'll wait down at the shack. Take your time, Amigo."

Will carefully unwrapped the package feeling and sensing the presence of Joaquina. The gift was a wind chime made of the hollow bones of eagle wings and pieces of finely molded, thin clay kachinas painted with elaborate designs and bead and feather work, all hanging from soft doeskin. Will tied it to the low hanging branch of the Aspen Billy had pointed to and then sat down next to the tree. The breeze caused the chime to sing the most delicate song of love that tugged at the heart strings as not even the Philharmonic Symphony could. Will remained there for some time looking out over the panorama spread below him, basking in the glorious feeling the soft melodic sounds the marriage of the wind and chimes had created. Finally, he took down the chimes, carefully returned them to the doeskin sheath, and started back down the hill to the shack feeling as good about himself and the world he lived in as he could ever remember feeling.

That evening, after a supper of broiled steaks and fried potatoes Billy took him down to the lake for a fishing lesson. Will had never heard of fly fishing with a plastic bubble and a spinning rod. He watched intently as Billy tied the bubble to his line and then added about six feet of leader and on the end of that a number sixteen mosquito. His second cast of no more than fifty yards brought a boiling on the surface as the tip of the pole bent under the attack of a two-pound rainbow trout. Billy quickly pointed his rod straight up and began to the play the bronzed-back warrior on the other end fighting for its life. Several times this determined denizen of deep water stripped line from the reel in an attempt to return to the safety of the depths, its brilliant colors flashing in the last rays of the setting sun as it broke the surface of the mirror-like waters of the lake. In the next thirty minutes Will enjoyed the success of Billy's lessons, and between them they had harvested no less than eight nice fat rainbow trout that would add a welcome change to both the breakfast and dinner menu tomorrow. It had been another halcyon day that Will would deposit deep into his bank of memories.

The next morning, with their bellies full of fresh fried trout washed down with strong coffee and eggs on the side, they saddled up and headed out to check the livestock. It was nearly noon when Billy ground-tied his gelding and beckoned for Will to join him.

"Look here, Will, we got some unwelcome company. See that paw print in that wet ground. I'd guess it's one big female puma. The female are always bigger than the toms and this one's mighty big. We haven't had any cats up here for several years and this is probably just one passing through on its way to another range. They migrate from time to time when the game gets scarce or a bigger cat or a grizzly moves into the neighborhood. But we best track it, if possible, and make sure. I doubt it'll bother the cows, but you never know, and I wouldn't want to be the one to tell Mr. Savage that I let a cat eat one of his cows."

The next three hours they lost and found the tracks at least a dozen times. The cat didn't appear to be hunting and, as Billy had suggested, it appeared to be heading across country at a steady pace and always in a southerly direction. This obvious straight direction allowed them to find the trail time and again when they lost it. Deciding they wanted to be back at the shack before dark, they headed back and came upon the cat's tracks again and again coming from due north, which reinforced Billy's theory that it was probably just passing through.

The next day they started early and attempted to get as accurate a count as possible to determine that all the cows were accounted for. By mid-afternoon they had pretty much concluded their combined counts confirmed that Will's efforts as a herder had been satisfactory, and Billy offered, "you just might make it as a cowherder after all, and I won't have to tell no lies to Mr. Savage about his summer cowpoke. I don't, however, intend to be honest with Joaquina. There's just no way I could tell her how lovesick a grown man has been actin'."

As they were heading back to the shack, Will was telling Billy how every evening he had seen a large flock of bats coming out of the rimrock and escarpment above camp. He pointed out a dark scar at the base of the cliff. When they got back to camp Billy dug out his binoculars and glassed the area Will had pointed out.

"Let's take a ride up there after supper and check it out. I'm no spelunker but there's bound to be a cave up there somewhere. I doubt those bats are livin' in a tree."

They arrived at the approximate area that Will thought the bats were coming from, ground tied the horses and traversed back and forth on foot looking for any hole in the escarpment that would serve as an entrance for the bats. It was on the third trip past an inconspicuous crack in the face of the lava rock that Billy detected a slight rush of cold air. Upon further investigation, he found the crack, hidden in the shadows, was considerably larger than it first appeared. He called Will over and showed him what he thought might be the entrance to a cave. He took a small flashlight he had brought along, and told Will to wait while he checked it out.

Waiting outside the cave entrance, Will Scanlon checked his watch again. How long had it been since Billy had slithered through the rock in the canyon wall and vanished into the darkness of their discovery? He had taken their only flashlight and suggested only one of them enter the cave, just in case.…

Will decided he would wait another ten minutes and then enter the cave in search of Billy. The sun would be setting soon, darkness would follow shortly, and they were several miles from the line shack.

Checking his watch for the tenth time in as many minutes, Will decided it was time. He had already spotted a pine tree nearby with some porcupine damage as a source of pine pitch he would need to fashion a torch. Taking a branch and his neckerchief wrapped in the sticky resin of the pine, he lit his torch, edged through the crack and into the chill wind blowing out of the cavern.

The passage-way was small and narrow, and it was necessary to crawl. He estimated he had gone about forty to fifty yards before he could stand again. The farther into the cave he crawled, the colder it seemed. Finally he was able to stand and lifting the torch high above his head, he saw what was the most astonishing, frightening, macabre sight his young eyes had ever witnessed.

He almost stumbled over Billy's body he was so absorbed in the totally unbelievable scene before him. It was immediately obvious that Billy Otero was no longer a member of the living. He was in a sitting position and in his hand, within a hand's reach of another departed soul, was a silver and turquoise bracelet. Billy's eyes were filled with horror and his mouth was gaping open. The flashlight lay on the ground, creating ghostly shadows on the cave wall.

What Billy had seen when he reached the point where he could stand was the answer to a secret that had been hidden for untold centuries. He had looked down a lava tube that reached into infinity which at some time in it's geologic history had become an ice cave and the burial ground for what appeared to be thousands of Anasazi. There they lay in all their ceremonial splendor, bedecked with ancient crafted jewelry, and spread about them, pottery and personal belongings worth a veritable fortune. An archaeological discovery the magnitude of King Tut's Tomb. After centuries they had not turned to dust, but due to the ice had remained in a mummified state. A similar discovery of frozen remains had recently been made in the Tyrolean Alps in Italy. Hunters discovered such a mummy frozen in a glacier. It was a shepherd with a stone dagger, a copper ax and a longbow and arrows. Scientific carbon dating placed his demise at fifty-three hundred years ago.

Billy, with his knowledge of the Anasazi and the traditions taught since early childhood, had felt as if he had entered the underworld of the dead and that the souls of his ancestors were all about him. He had reached down to the mummy nearest him and taken a beautiful silver and turquoise bracelet from the shrunken wrist. In doing so he had disturbed the corpse that had lain there for centuries. The bones of the other hand, with the skin turned to taut leather, moved and it had seemed to Billy with his superstitious leaning, that the mummy was reaching out to retrieve the bracelet. Billy Otero, who had been taught to respect the dead, knew fear that was so overwhelming, so intense, so totally terrifying he actually died of fright.

It happens. It has happened before and will happen

again. It is possible for the mind to override the physical being and shut it down, and all functions cease. The snow had not yet melted in the high country, the coyote whelps had not yet been weaned and those two fine young men, Alan Savage and Billy Otero were no longer counted among the living. The terrible prediction of Grandmother Maria had come to pass.

Will Scanlon in a near state of shock, both overcome by the magnitude of their discovery and the obvious departure from this world of his good friend, grabbed the flashlight lying at his feet and departed this house of horrors without looking back. Once outside in the lengthening shadows as the setting sun hurried the mountain toward darkness, Will tried to grasp what had taken place in the last few minutes. Between wrenching sobs, and suppressing the urge to scream, he gathered up the horses and headed back to the line shack.

The sun had been up for some time when Will finally quit his bedroll and managed to put down some coffee and a peanut butter sandwich, that was all he could think of for breakfast . He wasn't at all hungry, but knew he had to take on some degree of nourishment for the ugly task that lay before him this day. He didn't know how long he had slept because he had no way of knowing when he finally got to sleep. He had lain there for a long time, praying for strength and guidance, crying, cursing, first in fear and then in anger, and a host of conflicting feelings, until he was emotionally and physically exhausted. How could he break the news to Joaquina? What was he to do with this knowledge of ancient peoples that had been a mystery and secret for centuries? Why, of all the people in this world, had the burden of this knowledge been given him? Why had he been singled out? Why had Alan been killed in such a bizarre way? Why had Billy died such a horrible and premature death?

Will stood in the doorway looking out at the beautiful vista spread before him, the sun racing toward it's zenith in a cloudless cobalt sky, the pinion jays making a raucous noise, the only sound other then the near-silent murmurings of the aspen leaves in the slight breeze.

He could not put off any longer the ugly chore that lay before him. He must return to the cave and retrieve the body of Billy Otero, take it to the Johnson ranch and report his death.

The cold air escaping through the crack in the canyon wall seemed much colder than yesterday and the passageway seemed much longer. Finally, he reached the still-sitting figure of Billy. He took the bracelet from Billy's hand and for some inexplicable reason unbuttoned Billy's shirt pocket and placed the bracelet inside and buttoned the pocket again. Later, he had completely forgotten this act.

It was a difficult manuever to get the body of Billy with the rigor mortise settled in through the narrow passageway and out of the cave. The next problem was loading it on to a very skittish horse that was not about to cooperate. It became necessary to tie a hind leg of the horse up off the ground to the saddle horn in order to finally load on and tie down poor Billy.

Finally the trip down the mountain was started. Will was kept busy trying to put together the right words to tell Joaquina. He had gone no more than three or four miles when the skittish pack horse decided she had all that load she wanted and she reared and bolted, knocking Will out of his saddle and nearly unsaddling Will's horse as the lead rope burned it's way off the saddle horn. Will hit the ground on his back, knocking the wind out of his lungs. He watched helplessly as the pack horse raced off with Billy's remains. It was some time before he got his breath back. He had the presence of mind to hold tight to the bridle reins or surely there would have been two horses racing down the mountain. He tightened the cinch of his saddle, mounted and commenced the downhill trip once again. He hadn't gone far when he found pieces of the blanket he wrapped Billy in. They were hanging on a broken branch and there was considerable damage to several branches in nearby trees. Coming around a bend in the trail he came upon a grizzly sight. There lay the remains of Billy Otero sprawled across the top of a dwarfed pinion. The body of Billy had taken one terrible ride and apparently in an effort to get rid of its unwanted load, the horse had tried to scrape it off against every tree it passed. There was what was left of a branch at least half an inch in diameter protruding from Billy's side, another of the same size sticking out of his thigh, scratches on his face, and rips and tears in his shirt and trousers.

Will, with a set chin went about the ugly task of removing the branches that penetrated poor Billy's body and was surprised at the depth of the wounds and also at the lack of bleeding. Again it was necessary to tie up one of his horse's legs in order to load Billy's remains on the reluctant animal. Now it would mean Will would have to walk out leading his horse with its new passenger.

He had been on the trail about an hour when out of the corner of his eye he sensed movement below him. He stopped his horse and listened. His horse whinnied and pawed the ground nervously. A horse down the trail answered and about that time he could make out a horse and rider coming up the trail toward him. As they came near, he recognized old Mr. Johnson leading another saddled mount.

"Howdy, young man, looks like you run into trouble. I figured trouble when your pack horse came down the mountain with half the saddle gone."

"Thank God, it's you, Mr. Johnson. Billy Otero is

dead and I was bringing him down to the ranch when the horse took off. I found Billy tossed into the trees down trail and loaded him on my horse."

"We'll head on down, but first we'll tie that dead boy on Betty here. She's one gentle old mare and won't mind the smell of the dead. Most horses go crazy around dead bears and dead folks. I'm surprised you got this far."

As they were changing Billy's body from one horse to the other, Mr. Johnson spit out his ever-present wad of leaf tobacco, replaced it with an ample wad of fresh and said, "Afore I left the ranch I called Mr. Savage to let them know there was trouble. Got aholt of the missus. The old man and the Navajos was up in the timber cuttin' posts. She said she'd saddle up and go fetch them. I told her they had theirselves a might damaged horse with half a saddle and they might want a vet to work on the mare's cut-up foreleg. Gonna need stitches for sure. And son, when we get back to my place we'll off-load your friend Billy and then we'll be obliged to call the Sheriff's office. I don't know what happened here but I know what needs doin' in any accident, and they'll send out a deputy."

Back at the ranch, they off-loaded Billy's body and Mr. Johnson got a piece of dam canvas from the tack room. They laid the body in the shade and covered it with a couple of saddle blankets . Mr. Johnson went to the house to make that call to the Sheriff's office. Will unsaddled, rubbed down the horses and turned them loose in the corral. He saw what was left of the saddle Mr. Johnson had taken off and thrown over the top rail of the corral. It was missing a stirrup and fender, and the bridle had only one rein. He also saw where Mr. Johnson had put salve and some duct tape on the foreleg of the mare; the vet would need to look at that.

These chores taken care of, Will headed for the house,

trying to piece together in his mind just exactly what he was going to tell Joaquina.

Mr. Johnson saw him approaching the door and said, "Come in this house, young man. They're sending out a deputy and an ambulance to pick up the body. I got us some coffee brewin', be ready in a minute. S'pect you could use a cup 'bout now."

The Johnson house was as rustic as Old Man Johnson. A gigantic royal elk head hung above the native stone fireplace and an ancient muzzle loader rifle rested on a pair of deer legs made into a gun rack. On the opposite wall was an old rendition of the "End of the Trail", a pair of black sheepskin chaps and a braided leather lariat. The floors were bare flag stone except for two large red and black Navajo rugs. And, believe it or not, in the corner was an old upright Stromberg Carlson radio that was apparently still working. Will had quickly taken all this in as he looked for a telephone.

"Mr. Johnson, if you don't mind I'd like to use your phone. I should call Billy's sister and tell her what has happened here."

"Sure thing, son, there in the kitchen, you just help yourself and I'll pour us some coffee."

Will dug through his billfold and found the number at the Zuni reservation where he could reach Joaquina. The voice on the other end said she would get her and asked him to call back in ten minutes.

Will finished his second cup of coffee and dialed the number again. This time Joaquina answered. "Will is that you? What's wrong?"

With his throat so tight he could hardly manage a word he said, "Joaquina … He's gone, Billy's dead …

An awkward silence on both ends of the phone seemed to last forever. Finally, Joaquina said, "I some-how knew last night when Grandmother Maria acted so strange. I'm sure she knew, and then when your call came through I knew what your message would be."

The Sheriff's office is sending a deputy and an ambulance out. They'll be here soon. They'll need to be told instructions for disposition of the body."

Another awkward silence as Joaquina composed herself before she answered, "I'll get Grandmother Maria and we'll drive into Grants and meet you at the Sheriff's office."

"Oh Joaquina ... I'm so sorry. He just died; he just sat there and died."

"I know, Will ... perhaps Grandmother Maria understands ... perhaps we never will. We'll see you in town.

Will heard the line go dead as the phone on the other end was put in its cradle. As he turned he saw the Sheriff's car pulling into the yard with an ambulance not far behind.

DO NOT DISTURB
THE ANASAZI

The Sheriff's car came into the yard, made a sweeping turn in front of the house, and slammed on its brakes, kicking up a cloud of dust. As the deputy stepped out of the car, Old Man Johnson stepped off the front porch and yelled, "Just what the hell you think you're doin', this ain't no race track. Just cause you got funny lights on the roof of that car don't mean you can come tearin' into my yard. You hear what I said, little man?"

The "little man," was none other than Deputy Eppers. Old Man Johnson towered over him by at least a quarter of an inch. The Deputy was still wearing bandages on his disfigured ears, and his broken nose, and a cast on his hand.

Strange things happen in the course of events and the only reason Deputy Eppers had responded to the call for a deputy was that he was the only officer in the office when the call came through. Had it not been for the fact that Sheriff Ramirez had left for six weeks of training at the FBI school for law enforcement officers, the investigation of the Deputy would have now been completed and Eppers would probably be behind bars himself. Ramirez thought the medical leave of Eppers would last through the duration of his school and he had intended to complete the investigation on his return. But Eppers had returned to work immediately upon being dismissed from the hospital.

Eppers turned as red as the flashing lights on his car when he heard the diatribe from this little old rancher.

"I'm here to investigate an accidental death and I'm an officer on official business. You better mind your tongue old man."

"On my ranch I'm the only official and who you callin' and old man?

It was a Mexican standoff and the two of them just glared at one another waiting to see what would happen next. At this point, Will entered into the conversation. "The body's over here in the shade Deputy."

Eppers glared for a minute longer at the old rancher and then as close to a swagger as he could manage, headed for the body covered with saddle blankets. Upon removing the blankets, he immediately saw the scratches and the puncture wounds on Billy's body. He studied the deep wound in Billy's side assuming it might be the cause of death. He looked at Will and asked, "What happened here?"

Will said, "This is Billy Otero. He and I work for the Diamond G. We were up at the line shack and he died last night around six. I brought him down the mountain this morning."

Eppers looked at him suspiciously and asked again, "How'd he die?"

"He just died." was Will's reply.

Eppers asked, "Was anyone else around when he 'just died'?"

Will didn't like the tone or the direction these questions were heading and he looked directly at Eppers and said, "Just me and Billy, no one else, and I told you, he just died, just like that. Just what the hell are you inferring?"

Eppers reached behind his back with his one good hand and pulled out his hand cuffs, "I'm arresting you on suspicion of murder, turn around."

At this point Mr. Johnson intervened. "Don't be tryin' to put those bracelets on this young man....you hear what I'm sayin'? If you want him to come in and make a statement, I'll bring him to town. Now you get your puny little ass back in that county car and go on back to town afore I take me some advantage of a cripple."

Will thought the veins on the side of Eppers head would burst. His eyes were about to pop out of his head and he was swallowing as if a baseball was stuck in his throat. He turned and almost screamed at the ambulance driver, "Get that body loaded up and back to town. I'll get the coroner and we're gonna get us an autopsy and get to the bottom of this. " With that he stomped back to his car, slammed the door shut, ground the gears into low, put the gas pedal to the floor and laid a cloud of dust all the way back to the blacktop.

"C'mon son, I'll run you into town and we'll leave a message for the Diamond G folk. Might as well get this all straightened out, but I figured we didn't wanna do business with this fella. I've seen his kind afore and I'm here to tell ya, he's eight miles of bad road, little man with a big gun like he was carryin', why it's more dangerous than a diamondback."

They hadn't been gone long when Mr. Savage, Sarah and Justin pulled into the yard. They at once saw the note on the front screen door. Will had written on the yellow lined tablet paper Mr. Johnson had given him. He explained that Billy had died last night and while he was bringing the body down the pack horse bolted and knocked off Billy's body and ruined a saddle. He said he was under suspicion of murder by Deputy Eppers and that he and Mr. Johnson were going to the Sheriff's office. He added a postscript saying, "Billy just died, no accident, he just died."

Mr. Savage went into the house and looked around until he found the phone and the directory. He looked up the number for the District Attorney, dialed it and asked to speak to the D.A.

"Fred, this is Earl Savage, one of my hands, Will Scanlon, is on his way in to the Sheriff's office with Old Man Johnson. Billy Otero, another of my hands, died up at the line shack. His body is on its way to the coroner's office. That damned fool Eppers is trying to charge my hand with murder. We're leaving the Johnson ranch right now and I'd like you to meet me at the Sheriff's office." An apparent affirmative response on the other end and Mr. Savage hung up.

Back outside he said, "Justin, Sarah and me are headin' for town. Saddle up and mind the store at the line camp and we'll be in touch in a couple days, maas o menos. You might want to wait around for the vet and tell him to post me the bill."

When Mr. Johnson and Will came through the door to the Sheriff's office, Deputy Eppers was waiting for them. "I'm arresting you on suspicion of murder." And he proceeded to read him his rights, then turned to the clerk behind the desk and said, "Book him."

Mr. Johnson said he would wait for the Diamond G folk to get there, and they took Will away.

Joaquina and Grandmother Maria came into the office and Joaquina spoke to the clerk. "I'm Joaquina Otero, I understand they have brought the body of my brother here. Has Mr. Scanlon arrived yet?"

The clerk looked at her in surprise and said, "They have taken your brother's body to the morgue for an autopsy and Mr. Scanlon has been arrested for his murder."

"What are you saying? My brother has not been murdered and Will Scanlon has not murdered anybody."

At this point Mr. & Mrs. Savage came through the door and Joaquina went at once to Sarah, who took her in her arms.

Holding back the tears, Joaquina said, "Oh Sarah, a terrible thing is happening here. They say Billy has been murdered and that Will has killed him. I know this is not so. Grandmother Maria knows what has happened. Please help us."

Just then Deputy Eppers returned from the section where Will had been locked up. At the same time the District Attorney came through the door and walked towards Mr. Savage to shake his hand.

"Fred, thank goodness you're here. Get this mess straightened out. This sorry excuse for a deputy has assumed there's been a murder and that young Will Scanlon committed it. He's dead wrong on both counts and I want my hand released right now."

"Give me a minute, Earl. Let me discuss the events with the Deputy and see what we have in the way of evidence." With that he motioned for Eppers to follow him to the nearest office where they could discuss it further behind closed doors.

The District Attorney didn't like this Deputy Eppers

and he had a hard time trying to disguise these feelings. "Okay, Eppers, what do we have here?"

"Well, this Scanlon kid admits to being with Otero when he died, and I checked the body and there's a couple holes poked in it the size of a nightstick and I say it ain't no case of him just dyin'"

" That's it? That's all you got in the way of evidence? What's the Coroner say is the cause of death?"

Eppers was beginning to feel uncomfortable and in his own mind felt that there was politics involved here and that the owner of the Diamond G seemed to have a lot more influence then he should. "I think you oughta call him and find out for yourself."

With that the D.A. reached for the phone and dialed the Coroner. "Cecil this Fred, what can you tell me about the Otero boy they brought in, was it murder?

" Well, I've just begun the preliminaries and I can't say at this point. I can say there's strange things here. Supposedly, he died around six p.m. last night. Well, that doesn't appear to be the case, but it could be. The body appears to have been in a walk-in cooler or something, and there's some bodacious puncture wounds, but they all happened sometime after the body was dead. Without completing the autopsy and looking at all the organs I can't say for sure, but it looks at this point like the heart just stopped. I'll let you know as soon as I can confirm."

The D.A. hung up and said to Eppers, "You wait here, I'll be right back." And with that he asked to be taken to the cell where they were holding Will.

"Young man, I'm the District Attorney. Mr. Savage is out front and has asked me to help and I'll need to ask you some questions, if you don't mind. What happened there?" He was pointing to a bruise on the side of Will's face.

"That's a little gift from your deputy, he blind sided

me with a sap. No, I don't mind answering any questions. You can believe me or not, but I didn't kill Billy, he just died, and when I was bringing the body back down to Mr. Johnson's ranch the horse spooked and eventually managed to get rid of the body and part of a saddle. When I found the body, it was pretty beat up."

"Okay, that clears up some questions. Now tell me what time he died and was the body put in a spring house or cooler at the Johnson ranch?"

Will knew now that the temperature of the cave had skewed the time frame of events but decided to stay with the truth, with the exception of the discovery of the cave. "He died around six last night. He just simply died. We just put the body in the shade at the Johnson ranch, but it got pretty cold up on the mountain last night. Billy and I were the best of friends, were like brothers; in fact, in the not too distant future we were going to be brothers-in-law. I think your deputy has some serious problems with his authority."

"So do I, let's get you outa here. Guard, unlock this door, I'm releasing this prisoner."

When Will entered the room behind the D.A., Joaquina went to him at once and they embraced. Neither saying anything, just holding one another, sharing both grief and affection.

No sooner had he released Joaquina from his arms than Sarah was in them, saying, "Don't worry for a minute, Will. We're all here and we all know you haven't killed anyone."

The District Attorney took this as his cue and offered, "You're absolutely correct, Sarah. This young man is not being charged with anything. We'll wait for the Coroners report, but the preliminary report indicates death by natural causes. Now I've got to get back to my office and get to work."

It was Old Man Johnson who came up with the proper adjournment for this gathering, "There's the feller oughta be in jail where he can't cause hurt to innocent citizens." He was pointing at Eppers, who turned and stomped back to the locker room in the rear of the building.

But Eppers wasn't finished with this incident, hateful little man that he was. He drove over to the county coroner's office and asked to see the personal belongings of Billy Otero. Going through the pockets of his trousers, he found a billfold with a drivers license, three dollars, and some dog-eared business cards with phone numbers written on the backs. Going through the shirt pocket, he found the silver and turquoise bracelet and knew at once it was ancient and valuable. He guessed they had robbed a grave and began to put together a plan.

Outside the Sheriff's office Mr. Savage told Will, "We're all sorry about what happened here. It's a shame that Billy's unfortunate death has caused us further suffering and hurt because of an ugly little man that hides behind the authority of that badge. If you need to take some time off, Will, it's all right. I've got Justin lookin' after things at the line camp."

"No, if it's all right with you I'd like to head back up there early in the morning. Meanwhile, I want to spend some time with Joaquina and Grandmother Maria.

Sarah entered the conversation, seizing the opportunity to have a house full of company again. "Why don't we all go out to the ranch and I'll fix dinner. "We've plenty of room and Grandmother Maria can have the guest room. Then tomorrow morning we can drive Will over to the Johnson ranch."

All were in accord and Sarah couldn't have been more pleased. She thrived on a house full of company. She was at her very best when she could cook for her extended family. She needed these gatherings to fill a void left by Alan's death.

That evening after dinner Will asked Grandmother Maria if she would take a walk with him. They hadn't gone far when Grandmother Maria said, "Will, I want you to know, I have seen what you have seen, I know you have found the Anasazi, I know how Billy died, I know all these things, not by my own choosing, these things have been made known to me. I have told Joaquina you are pure of heart, this I believe. I hope Billy didn't die for no cause. I hope you will honor his memory with your silence. I must warn you that to dishonor the dead is a terrible guilt to take to the grave, but even worse is the many years one may have to live with this guilt. I know there is a fortune to be made for those who would rob the dead. But how do you measure wealth? Truly, not by dollars. The man who has my Granddaughter's love is richer by far than the richest man as measured by gold and silver. I give you good counsel, Will Scanlon. Be satisfied with riches money cannot buy, be thankful for all you have been given. Keep this secret locked in your heart and share it with no one. Your reward will be great, I promise you."

This was not at all what Will had expected. They walked on in silence, almost to the first cattle guard, then turned in unison and started back toward the house. The sun had long since fallen behind the western horizon. With the lengthening shadows a breeze had come up and with it a coolness that seemed to penetrate to Will's bones. He shivered and reached out to take Grandmother Maria's hand…, ancient, wrinkled old hand gnarled with the disfiguring of arthritis but radiating a warmth that seemed to reach out and possess him. He sensed a power in her that could not be denied.

When they were almost to the house he broke the

silence, "Grandmother Maria, I loved Billy as a brother and you must know how deeply I love Joaquina. I have never taken my blessings for granted. I give thanks every day for my wealth, which I have never measured in dollars. I am grateful for your good counsel and your faith in me and I am especially grateful for your friendship. I will not place it in jeopardy."

The next morning as they were dropping Will off at the Johnson ranch, Joaquina said to Will, "Whatever was it you said to Grandmother last night? She tells me this morning she has taken you into her heart and that she will bless our union."

Will replied, "It was more what she said. I mostly listened, she was doing most of the talking."

It would be good to be back at the line shack and sort things out and grieve the loss of Billy in private. Mr. Savage had driven over an extra pick-up for Justin and he could head back in the morning. Joaquina seemed to understand Will's wish not to attend Billy's funeral. It would be a simple ceremony and he would be put to rest in the Savage family plot next to Alan.

As he reined his horse up-trail, storm clouds were gathering over the Divide and sheet lightning flashed in the distance. Will welcomed the rain that would clean the earth. At least until the next storm.

THE ANASAZI'S REVENGE

Justin heard Will's approach while he was still in the timber at the north end of the lake. He quietly saddled a horse and moved into the shadows in the Aspen waiting to see who was coming. When he saw it was Will coming out of the timber he rode out to meet him. "How goes it, Will? Did you escape or are you free on bond or did they decide to hang the Deputy?"

"Good to see you Justin, old friend, no, the Coroner confirmed that Billy died of natural causes. I know there's no dignity in death, but Billy's passing deserved better than this, dragging the family down to the Sheriff's office and talking about the body's condition in front of everyone. It was unnecessary and all because of that stinkin' little puke of a man. Joaquina is holding up surprisingly well but I'm not so sure about Sandy. She and Billy were getting pretty serious. Well, it's over and life belongs to the living. I've got to sort things out and try to accept what's happened and ... enough of this .... what do you need to tell me about my cows so you can head back down to the ranch?

Justin knew when silence was the best response and they rode quietly back to the line shack where Justin went about gathering up his few pieces of gear to start down the mountain.

He was no sooner out of sight than Will felt as alone as he could remember. There wasn't breeze enough to disturb the aspen leaves and the lake was like a mirror. The sun was reaching its zenith and there wasn't a cloud in the sky. The only movement disturbing this tranquil scene was a lone turkey vulture soaring silently, high over the lake making wider and wider circles. Will watched him for some time and then whispered, "Billy, old friend, if that's you up there you must surely know how you'll be missed." And as he said it he felt his throat tightening up and a tear ran down his cheek. He swallowed hard, turned abruptly and headed for his horse, stepped into the saddle and reined his horse toward the south to check the cattle.

It was the next morning when Deputy Eppers drove into the Johnson ranch. Old Man Johnson was coming from the hay barn when he saw the car pull up alongside the corral. When Deputy Eppers got out from behind the wheel, Johnson was first curious and then angry and his anger must have been obvious as he approached Eppers.

Eppers put up his hand saying, "Now take it easy Johnson, this isn't official business, I'm here askin' for a favor. I need to rent one of your horses. young Scanlon has invited me up to the lake at the line shack for some fishin'. You may not believe me but he and I had a long talk and are tryin' to put this mess behind us."

Old Man Johnson looked at him for some time, spit

out a wad of his ever-present tobacco, wiped the juice off his chin with an already-soiled shirt sleeve, took off his sweat-stained ancient Stetson, wiped the sweat band and his forehead with his bandanna, and reached into his hip pocket for another wad of tobacco.

He finally spoke, "you're right about that, I may not believe it. Why that boy would want to spend any time with you is beyond my ken. But then the decent ones don't always seem to have good sense."

And after another long pause, "Well I reckon as how I can rent you a horse and tack, but here's the conditions that go along with it. You leave that cannon you're packin' in your car. If you ain't back by day after tomorrow I'm gonna go deer huntin' early this year. You hear what I said, little man?"

Old Man Johnson saddled up a gentle old mare for the deputy, gave him directions to the line camp, watched him out of sight and then headed back to the hay barn, feeling rather uncomfortable about the morning's events.

Several times during the day Will felt as if he were not alone and knew his horse was acting uneasy. He wondered if perhaps the cat was back in the country. He had the uneasy feeling all day that someone or some thing was watching him. That night he levered a round into the chamber of the Winchester Mr. Savage had insisted he take with him, and leaned it against the wall next to the door. He put in a restless night of half asleep and half awake and was up early at the first color in the east. After breakfast, as he saddled his horse he strapped on the rifle scabbard, and along with his lunch added binoculars to the saddle bag. It was near noon when he rode toward the escarpment and the cave. He ground-tied his horse near the hidden entrance and looked long and hard at the outcropping above the entrance and the ridge line on top. He retrieved the binoculars from the saddle bag, stepped back about sixty yards or so and continued to glass the ridge line above the cave. Walking back to his horse he replaced the binoculars and took out his lunch of sliced bologna wrapped in flour tortillas with green chiles. He settled himself on a rock and was enjoying the warmth of the noonday sun, trying to make a decision about the sleeping souls just beyond the basalt barrier that separated them. His horse pawed the ground nervously and again he had that sensation that they were being watched. Once as he was getting his canteen from the saddle bags, he thought he saw a flash of light in a copse of scrub oak. He continued to watch that area for some time, appearing not to do so, and finally convinced himself he was imagining things. Eventually he stepped back into the saddle and headed back toward the line shack.

Deputy Eppers watched him for some time making sure he was heading back to camp. He was tired and hungry and not happy about spending the night on a bed of pine needles worrying whether or not he had tied his horse secure enough. The few sandwiches he had brought along had long since left an aching hole in his gut and he was cussing himself for not coming better prepared. A drink from a seep from a hidden spring had sufficed but did not begin to fill his belly that was conditioned to a rather large breakfast of a morning.

Satisfied that Scanlon was out of sight and hearing, he moved his horse toward the cliff wall where Will had tied his horse. Eppers tied his horse in the same area and began a concerted search of the rock formation. It was on his third swing of the compass when he sensed the cool breeze coming from the rock wall. Upon further investigation he found the crack and the cold air coming from within. He returned to his horse and dug through his little pack for a flashlight he had at least had the foresight to bring.

Once inside he couldn't believe the magnitude of his discovery, and began to calculate the fortune in ancient jewelry spread out before him. He actually began to slobber and his breathing turned in to frantic panting as greed all but consumed him. He moved quickly from one mummified corpse to the other, relieving them of the priceless possessions that had been interred with them. He immediately put together a plan to take as much now as he could carry, kill young Scanlon and then leave the country and return at a later date to harvest it all.

In his greed and his haste he dropped his flashlight and the delicate bulb shattered on the frozen floor of the cave. Eppers panicked and tried to orient himself with the probable opening of the cave and stumbled over one of the disturbed Anasazi, falling forward upon the raised skeletal hand from which he had just removed a bracelet. A hand that reached out from centuries of rest undisturbed until now.

A sickening sound echoed through the dark, cold chamber as the bony fingers penetrated the throat of this robber who had dared to disturb their sleep. Perhaps it was stark terror or shock that allowed the body of this greedy little man to simply lay there while his life blood flowed out onto the cold icy floor of this darkened tomb.

It was almost noon and Will had just returned from an inspection of the cattle that had been grazing along the southern boundary of the lease when he was mysteriously drawn to return to the cave. He couldn't account for the strange feeling that seemed to pull him like a magnet toward the escarpment. As he came within sight of the cave entrance, he saw the horse tied in front and upon further investigation saw the brand on the left rear was Old Man Johnson's Lazy J. Once again he fashioned a torch, making use of the pine tar oozing out of the porcupine damaged tree, and entered, albeit reluctantly, the resting place of the Anasazi.

As he reached the end of the narrow passageway where he could stand, he held his torch high and took in the grizzly sight of Deputy Eppers impaled on the lifeless hand that had reached out of the past to claim revenge for this trespass on the sleeping Anasazi. The flickering shadows from the torch added a ghostly aura to this macabre scene. Will shivered involuntarily and felt a cold that seemed to make his blood turn to ice. He took one last look at this pathetic person whose eyes reflected stark terror and appeared to be bulging from their sockets, then made an instant decision and exited posthaste this house of horrors.

Once outside, he gulped in the fresh air scented with pine and felt the warmth of the sun once again. He stood there for some time, numbed from the ugly scene he had just left. Finally he initiated his decision. He would leave Epper's body untouched. It seemed almost sacrilegious to leave this scum buried in what was surely hallowed ground. But that was his decision. He would return tomorrow and implement his plan to hike to the top of the ridge line and displace enough of the large boulders to conceal forever the resting place of the Anasazi and the piece of human trash that now resided with them.

He started down the mountain trailing Johnson's mare behind and found Old Man Johnson sitting on the corral fence looking up the trail. As Will dismounted Johnson spit tobacco into the corral and said, "I was just fixin' to head up your way."

Will lifted the pole of the corral gate, led the mare in and commenced to unsaddle her. "I found your mare up by the line shack Mr. Johnson and figured you'd be lookin' for her."

Old Man Johnson getting down off the fence said, "Didn't see the dude that rode her up there did you?"

"Nope, just your mare, "replied Will.

About a week later an article in the local paper reported the results of Sheriff Ramirez' completed investigation of Deputy Eppers, stating that he had evidently fled to avoid prosecution.

EPILOGUE

It was years later when Joaquina's husband, a successful young archaeologist, told his sister of the discovery of the **Dead of Chaco Canyon,** but not the location.